A NEST IN THE
ASHES

A NEST IN THE ASHES

Christine Goff

WHEELER
CHIVERS

This Large Print edition is published by Wheeler Publishing, Waterville, Maine USA and by BBC Audiobooks, Ltd, Bath, England.

Published in 2004 in the U.S. by arrangement with The Berkley Publishing Group, a member of Penguin Group (USA) Inc.

Published in 2004 in the U.K. by arrangement with The Berkley Publishing Group, a member of Penguin Putnam Inc.

U.S. Softcover   1-58724-642-2 (Cozy Mystery)
U.K. Hardcover   0-7540-9661-0 (Chivers Large Print)
U.K. Softcover   0-7540-9662-9 (Camden Large Print)

The text of this Large Print edition is unabridged.
Other aspects of the book may vary from the original edition.

Set in 16 pt. Plantin by Minnie B. Raven.

Printed in the United States on permanent paper.

British Library Cataloguing-in-Publication Data available

ISBN 1-58724-642-2 (lg. print : sc : alk. paper)

To Janet Grill, for always being there to give me the speech. You truly are a sister of my heart.

Acknowledgments

Several people helped me to bring this story to life, by providing technical information. My deepest thanks to: Bill Maron and Pete Anderson, old friends and firefighters extraordinaire, who were kind enough to supply me with insider info; Jeff Connor and Jesse Duncrack of the National Park Service Fire Management Offices; Tasha Kotliar, USGS, who is studying the effects of fire on avian populations; and Ronda Woodward, an amazing birder who helped me spot my first green-tailed towhee.

Additional thanks goes to my fellow writers and friends who supported me through the process. To my RMFW buddies, you know who you are; to members of my critique group who made me go back and work the material again, and again, and again, ad nauseam — Bob Strange, Diane West, Janene McCrillis, Suzanne Proulx, Steven Moores, Georgeanne and Steven Nelson, Janice Ford, Louise Woodward, James Faber, and Gwen Schuster-Haynes; and to the WRW Retreaters, especially Janet Chapman, Jan Chalfant, Rhonda Foster, John Getze, Roman White, Jason Sitzes, Loren Oberweger, and

Gail Stockwell who offered encouragement during the soggy middle.

And to my family and friends, without whose support I'd be nothing: Mardee, Danielle, and Addie, who ate too much take-out; Mike, Krista, Hunter, Kayla, Gin, Kenny, Cherie, and Travis, who offered support from a distance; Tom, Monk, and Laura Ware; Aunt D, Cynthia, and Aja; and my beloved and beleaguered husband, Wes Goff.

Finally, I'd like to thank my editor, Cindy Hwang, for her unwavering confidence and patience; Peter Rubie, my favorite agent; Georgie Nelson and Mike Milligan, for the dynamite website; and Ann Elphick, my publicist, for helping me feed the birds.

Chapter 1

A flicker of orange caught Eric's attention, and he squinted toward a small stand of bitterbrush some fifty yards southeast of the turnaround. Under the cover of branches, a green-tailed towhee foraged in the grass.

He knew the bird, even without his binoculars. A classic double-scratcher, it jumped forward, then back, searching the dirt for insects and seeds.

The towhee turned, its rust-colored cap aflame in the sunlight. Then, as if sensing the danger, it darted back into the safety of the shrub.

Eric walked toward the back of his pickup and triggered the mike on his handheld radio. "Devlin, do you copy? Over." He enunciated carefully, worried that his Norwegian accent might garble his words on the airwaves. It was important Wayne Devlin understood who was calling.

No answer.

"Devlin, what's your ETA? Over." *Come on, Wayne. Where are you?*

Silence. Not even a burst of static.

"Give it up, Linenger." Nora Frank brushed past him and hoisted herself into the bed of a nearby National Park Service truck. Crawling forward, regulation-green pants stretched tight across her rear end, she hauled out a box of fusees. "Devlin's AWOL, again. And if experience is any indicator, he'll most likely stay that way."

"AWOL?" After seventeen years of living in the United States, it surprised Eric that there were still some American expressions he didn't know.

"Absent without Leave," she explained, sitting and dangling her feet from the tailgate of the truck. "Which, I point out, as Wayne's second-in-command, puts *me* in charge."

Now there is a frightening thought.

Eric stepped closer. "Does that mean the burn is still on?"

Surprise flickered across her face. "You bet. As far as I'm concerned, it's a go."

He had expected the answer, had even braced himself for it, so he managed not to curse out loud. Annoying her would only complicate matters.

Nora smirked.

Had she picked up on his struggle to keep his mouth shut?

Pulling two paper-wrapped fusees out of the box, she deftly linked them together and measured the length against the side of her leg. "Look long enough?"

Eric shook his head, not that he wanted her to continue construction. "You're short."

"Yeah," she drawled. "And you're tall."

"That's not what I meant." He picked up a fusee, spun it in his hand, then pressed circles into his open palm with the coupling end. "Is there any way I can convince you to call off the burn?"

Nora grinned, added another fusee to the chain she was working on, then pointed it toward the far end of the turnaround. "You don't cancel a party once the guests have arrived."

"Wayne would," he mumbled.

Still, Eric realized she had a point. The staging area teemed with people. Butch Hanley, the holding boss, held court from a picnic bench, doling out assignments to Nomex-clad personnel — a mixture of Elk Park Fire Department volunteers and trained NPS employees — responsible for containment of the fire within the prescribed perimeters.

Beyond them, Ernie Beal, the burn's ignition specialist, hunkered down in the grass with the two firefighters responsible for lighting the burn. Near the tanker, Howard Stevens, the fire observer, pored over burn maps with several people from Intermountain Regional NPS. And, from the meadow, a woman with a cameraman in tow shot footage of the operation.

"We've got the manpower, and the equipment," said Nora. "The hoses are laid. The

11

hand lines are dug. Not to mention we've sunk six thousand dollars into this burn, before even lighting the sucker." Nora shrugged. "Besides, Pacey Trent's here to watch the show." Setting aside the joined fusees, she reached back into the box. "You can sweet-talk me all you want, Linenger, but I'm giving the order to go."

Eric frowned. Was this the same woman who'd once shared his passion for the woods?

He'd met her four years ago at a National Park Service party held at Wayne Devlin's house. She was fresh out of training — enthusiastic, energetic, and idealistic. He'd factored in her dark wavy hair, blue eyes, and the smattering of freckles splashed across her nose and cheeks, and decided she was perfect girlfriend material.

Fortunately, it didn't take long to figure out that beneath the wholesome image lay a bobcat determined to rise to the top of the food chain. But, up until now, her ideals had held strong.

"Whatever happened to preserving habitat, Nora?"

"Oh cut the melodrama, already. Trust me, the bitterbrush and sage *will* grow back. The towhees and warblers *will* return. Hey, in three or four years, you'll be hard-pressed to prove there ever was a burn."

"*Ja?* Have you forgotten about the herbivary? New shoots may come up, but they'll be ravaged by the elk." Eric clamped his hands on the rail of the pickup. Why couldn't she see what they were doing?

"At least tell me you read my report," he said.

"I read it. Your concerns were duly noted, considered, and . . ." She placed her finger alongside her cheek and looked toward the sky before fixing him with a hard stare. "Denied."

Eric banged his fist against the truck's wheel well.

Nora ignored him. "So, where do you suppose Devlin is?" she asked.

Eric wished he knew. As Rocky Mountain National Park's fire management officer, Wayne Devlin was the only one besides Nora Frank or Pacey Trent with the power to stop the burn. Wayne should have been on the job hours ago.

"Your guess is as good as mine," replied Eric. "I don't know why he isn't answering the radio, unless he's somewhere out of range."

"Did you try calling Jackie?"

He nodded. "I talked to her around eight o'clock. She said he left before six this morning, mumbling something about too much fuel on Eagle Cliff Mountain." Eric shrugged. "Maybe he's reconsidering."

Nora chuckled. "I wouldn't hold my breath if I were you."

13

"*Ja,* well, as long as there's hope." It was the only straw left to grasp.

"*Ja,* well," she singsonged, mimicking his accent, "take my advice. Chill out, and go with the flow."

Eric gritted his teeth. Too bad she wasn't a man. He wouldn't mind decking her.

"Nora Frank?" called out a booming voice.

Nora straightened and smiled at someone behind Eric. "Good morning, Mr. Trent."

Eric turned around to find the Intermountain Regional NPS fire management officer storming toward them like a charging grizzly. At fifty-something, his brown hair shot with silver, the FMO walked hunched over as though still humping a firefighter's pack. A gigantic man, he stood six-foot eight, dwarfing Eric by half a foot.

"Where in the hell is Devlin?"

"We don't know," replied Nora, sliding onto her feet from the tailgate. "Sir," she added. "We just tried raising him on the radio. He didn't answer."

Eric winced at her use of "we." Being lumped into a category with Nora made him nervous.

Trent pointed at Eric. "Try him again."

Eric keyed the mike on his handheld. "Come in, Devlin. Over."

The radio crackled, and Eric strained to pick out words among the hisses and

14

squawks. "Wayne, is that you? This is Linenger. Over."

A responding burst of static fueled Eric's hopes. "Did anyone else copy that?"

"No," responded a voice from his radio.

"Nope."

"No."

"Has anyone seen him?" asked Eric.

Another volley of negative replies hammered home Eric's burgeoning headache. "Look, Devlin, if you can hear me, you're needed at the main staging area, immediately. Over."

Nothing.

"He must still be out of range," said Eric, afraid to voice his real concern — that something worse had happened. Wayne had disappeared with no explanations a few times in the past, and Nora was keeping score. Give her too many incidents to report, and Wayne would be out of a job.

"Yeah, or maybe he's out to breakfast," muttered Nora.

Trent's eyes narrowed. "Ms. Frank, would you care to explain that comment?"

Nora skimmed her hands along her hips, brushed nonexistent dirt from the seat of her fire pants. "Let's just say, Wayne Devlin is getting more and more unpredictable. There are days, like today, when he doesn't even bother to show up."

She scooped up the pile of fusees, and

Trent reached for the bundle. "Here, let me help you with those."

Nora rewarded him with a smile.

"If what you say is true, it sounds like we've got a problem." Trent lit out across the parking lot, and Eric and Nora fell in sync, one on either side of him.

"Mr. Trent, Wayne usually has a reason for not coming in," said Eric. He knew he sounded defensive. And he'd stretched the truth. The bottom line was, Wayne hadn't been acting much like himself lately.

"Either way, we can't afford to stand around here all day. Every second we do costs the Park Service money. Who's in charge when Devlin's gone?"

"I am, sir," said Nora.

"Good. Then let's get this show on the road."

Thirty minutes later, with the sun beating down from a cloudless sky, Ernie Beal lit the first fusee, and Eric resigned himself to the burn. He'd done his best to stop it, done everything possible to convince Nora to change her mind. He'd even tried calling Wayne at home one more time. His wife, Jackie, still hadn't heard from him. Now all Eric could do was try to minimize the damage.

So far, things looked good. The humidity had bottomed out at fifteen percent, and winds, drifting out of the west at one to five miles per hour, had nudged the temperatures into the forties. By all accounts, it was the perfect day for a fire. Just enough breeze to push four-inch flames through the bitter-brush.

Pulling a ragged breath, Eric gazed out over Beaver Meadows. Composed mostly of big sagebrush, antelope bitterbrush, and grasses, the meadow spread to the east and south, blanketing the valley floor in pale green shrubs. Along its southern edge, the meadow thinned, becoming understory for the ponderosa pines, before giving way to the dense stands of Douglas fir and spruce that climbed Eagle Cliff Mountain's north face.

In two days, it would all be char. *What a waste!*

Eric flinched watching the fire bite in the grass. Brush shriveled against the advancing heat. Smoke spiraled into the air, hazing the view of Longs Peak.

The flames grew in intensity, searing the air, and lapping forward through the grass and sage in speeds up to seventeen chains. At this rate, the fire would consume nearly two acres an hour.

Helpless to prevent the holocaust, he focused on the task at hand. As RMNP's fire monitor, it fell in his lap to track the fire's progress. If the fire ran ahead too quickly, it was his job to notify Butch Hanley and slow things down. If the fire slopped over its boundaries, Eric would scream for more manpower. If it threw spots, he would report the location, then report to the scene.

Bottom line? It was his job to avert disaster.

It took six minutes for the flames to flush the green-tailed towhee. Other birds and animals followed. Drab-colored Virginia's warblers darted here and there. Rabbits hopped. Mice scurried. Two dove-gray loggerhead shrikes with black wings flashed white-wing patches in retreat, and brownish-gray house finches in bright red plumage escorted their mates to safety. It was like a scene out of *Bambi*.

"Lookin' good," said the woman he'd seen earlier in the meadow. She signaled to her cameraman, who stepped around her, then she moved in beside Eric.

"Excuse me, ma'am. This is a restricted area."

"Press." She flashed a picture credential showing bleached hair and a toothy smile. "Linda Verbiscar, KEPC-TV." She stuck out her hand.

Eric hesitated, then shook. "Eric Linenger, National Park Service."

"Mind if I ask you a few questions?" On her signal, the cameraman tipped back his cap and trained the camera on Eric's face.

Eric held up an arm and turned sideways. "I'm a little busy right now."

"What about freedom of the press?" she asked, producing a microphone. "We're live in five, four, three, two, one." She turned to face the camera. "Hello, Dan. We're live on the scene of the first prescribed burn of the season here in Rocky Mountain National Park, and we're talking with Eric Linenger of the National Park Service. Tell us, Mr. Linenger, what is the reason for today's fire?"

Eric glanced nervously at the camera. Nothing like being put on the spot. "The intent is to burn off a thousand acres of dense vegetation."

"Why? To what *purpose?*"

"Strictly preventative. By removing the fuel, we hope there will be less risk of catastrophic wildfire."

Linda turned to face the camera, and Eric tried edging away. Verbiscar placed her hand on his arm. "A quick explanation for our viewers, Dan. Since 1910, when a fire known as 'the Big Blowup' consumed three million acres of forest and killed eighty-five people in Idaho and Montana, fire suppression has been the policy of the federal government. In fact, by the 1970s, vigorous firefighting efforts had knocked the number of consumed acres from fifty million to five million a year."

So far she had the facts right.

"But now, natural fuels have accumulated in our forests, creating tinderbox conditions, and specialists recommend thinning them through

19

the reintroduction of fire. The hope is, that by returning the forests to a more natural, fire-resistant state, the forests will burn more or less as nature intended them to."

She turned back to Eric. "What I'd like to know is, in the wake of the Cerro Grande prescribed burn near Los Alamos . . . a fire which jumped its prescribed boundaries, burned over forty-five thousand acres, destroyed two hundred thirty-five homes, and caused eighteen thousand people to be evacuated . . . how do you justify taking the risk?" She shoved the microphone in Eric's face.

He swallowed. "We've had successful fires since the Cerro Grande."

Linda Verbiscar smiled. "Yes, but how do you *personally* feel about prescribed burning?" She held up a copy of his report recommending against the Beaver Meadows prescribed burn. "Didn't you state in an advisory report that this particular fire was a mistake?"

Eric glanced at the line of fire advancing across the meadow. "Yes, but not because I don't believe in burning."

"Then why?"

"Because it's the only prime habitat within the park that supports green-tailed towhees and Virginia's warblers."

His response caused her to pause, then she turned back to the camera. "Well, there you have it, Dan. According to Eric Linenger, fire is bad for the bird population."

"That's not —"

She stepped away from him, anchoring a view of the fire behind her left shoulder. "That's all from the scene. We'll keep you apprised of any unusual developments. Now, it's back to you in the studio, Dan." Verbiscar plastered a smile on her face and tapped her toe five times. "And clear." She signaled a wrap to the cameraman, and stuffed the microphone back in her coat pocket. "Let's head down to the containment area."

"Excuse me, Ms. . . .Verbiscar," said Eric. "You misquoted me. I never said fire was bad for all birds."

"No? That's what I heard you say. Isn't that what you heard, Charlie?"

The cameraman nodded.

"What I said was, that this particular fire is bad for two species of birds. There are other species that thrive in burned-out areas."

She tucked a strand of bleached hair behind her ear. "Well, I'm glad we clarified that. Let's go." She signaled to the cameraman, who headed along the road.

Eric had started after them, when a gust of wind kicked up a dust devil, spitting dirt and gravel against the back of his legs.

Gusts hadn't been predicted.

He stared out at the fire. Then, amidst a shower of embers, a three-foot flame shot into the air.

Chapter 2

The wind freshened, driving hard out of the northwest, swirling ash, spark, and smoke from the blackened area into the unburned shrubs of the meadow. Sagebrush and bitterbrush erupted in fire. Flames rose in leaping columns, rolling through the grass in waves of orange and red, like a flash flood, headed straight for Eagle Cliff Mountain.

This is bad.

Eric scanned the tree line in the distance. If the fire grabbed hold in the ponderosa, the whole mountain would go up in flames. "Butch, do you copy?"

The handheld radio squawked. "Yo."

"We've got a situation here."

"*Tell* me about it." The stress in Butch Hanley's voice was audible. "Where the hell did this wind come from? Didn't Nora check the weather forecast before giving the go?"

"Of course I did," snapped Nora, her voice heating the airwaves.

Eric looked, but didn't see her at the turnaround. She must have followed the crew down to the other staging area.

"This wasn't on the menu," she said.

"Yeah?" replied Butch. "Well now it's the

blue plate special."

After a beat, she asked, "So, guys, tell me, where do we stand?"

"We've dug a three-foot hand line in front of the trees, but . . ." Butch's voice trailed off, and Eric raised his binoculars, panning the far edge of the meadow until he located the holding boss through the lenses. Butch mopped his face with a handkerchief. "At the speed this fire's moving," he said, "we ain't stoppin' it here."

"He's right," said Eric. By his own estimate, the rate of burn had jumped to over one hundred chains — or ten acres — an hour. The fire would hit the hand line in under forty minutes; the Visitor Center in a little over an hour. "We need to order a water drop now."

"No!" declared Nora. "We're not wasting resources unless we have to."

Eric watched a gust of wind bolster the flames. The fire surged forward. Adrenaline urged him to action, but he could do nothing to curb the onslaught of flames. "We can't afford to wait. We have no other option."

"Sure we do," said Nora. "The crew can run a black line next to the hand line. That'll give us a six-foot buffer, and hopefully buy us —"

"Are you nuts?" hollered Butch. "We'll just be adding more fire."

"Yeah, well, do it," she ordered. "I'll have

23

Bernie light a backfire to suck air from the burn. Hopefully, that will slow this puppy down. Butch, you have the remaining crews narrow the field by forcing the burn in on either side. Then, when the fire reaches the trees, put everyone on the line." Nora paused. "We can contain this sucker."

"It's too risky," Eric insisted. Smoke clouded the valley, stinging his eyes, burning his nose. She needed to act now. "I say —"

"Hey, Mr. Linenger," bellowed Linda Verbiscar, clambering back from the road with cameraman Charlie in tow. Eric greeted her with his back.

"— call in the chopper," he finished.

"No!"

Eric shivered through his sweat. "You're making a mistake, Nora."

"It's my decision."

The radio fell silent. All Eric could hear was the roar of the fire, like a train barreling along at high speed. One bump, and the train derails. "You're right," he said. "It's your call. But I think you're making a mistake."

"Duly noted."

Another silence, then the radio hissed and Butch Hanley's voice broke the tension. "Okay, then, I'll get the crew on it."

Eric signed off. After drawing a deep breath, he turned to Linda Verbiscar. She was peering at him through dark, wide set eyes rimmed with heavy eyeliner. Mascara, softened by the heat of the fire, puddled on her face, creating dark circles under her eyes. Red lipstick spidered into the crevices around her mouth. She looked melted. Yet, oddly, despite the wind, her hair remained perfectly coifed.

"What are they planning to do?" she asked, signaling Charlie to keep filming the fire.

A spate of orders burst from the radio. Eric turned down the volume. "They're going to put it out."

"How?"

He stared out at the fire, his gaze resting on the charred bush where the towhee had nested, and explained Nora's plan.

"Will it work?"

"Off the record?" He didn't really trust the woman, but he wasn't going to lie.

Verbiscar hesitated. "Sure."

"I don't know."

As much as Eric hated to admit it, Nora's plan seemed to be working. Within an hour, the backfire had slowed the pace of the original burn by fifty chains, Butch Hanley's black line had widened the buffer zone to six feet, and the crews had narrowed the burn considerably. Now, as everyone stood ready to defend the line, all any of them could do was hope the efforts were enough.

Eric scanned the edge of the meadow with his binoculars. Several spot fires smoldered in the bordering trees, and soot-streaked fire-fighters hustled to contain them. Fire lapped at brown bark. Chain saws buzzed. Shouts, and the crack of Pulaskis striking wood, echoed across Beaver Meadows.

Seconds later, Howard Stevens, the fire observer, loomed into view in the lenses, his shoulders blotting out the fire scene as he scribbled notes into a small, ringed binder, recording every detail of what happened — down to who did what, when, where, and on whose authority. If Nora was lucky, her plan would work. If not, a written record would detail everything she'd done wrong.

As Eric watched the fire sweep toward the line, a gust of wind rocked him forward, onto his toes. The wind lifted ash and embers from the meadow floor, curled them into a fist, and delivered a blow to the flames. Men and women scattered. The wind howled through the valley. Fire rocketed into the trees.

Chapter 3

A gust of wind buffeted the deck of the Warbler Café, yanking a paper plate out of Lark
Drummond's hand. The plate soared like a
Frisbee into the parking lot, spewing jelly
and half-eaten scones like sparks off a pinwheel. A to-go cup teetered, then tipped over
on a nearby table, splashing lukewarm coffee
across the plastic surface and onto the redwood deck. Napkins danced in the air like
overgrown confetti.

Lark eyed the mess with dismay. *What a
disaster!*

Adding to the ambience, the Park Service
had been burning in Rocky Mountain National Park since 9 a.m. In under an hour,
the smell of charred grass and pine pollen
had saturated the air. To the west, a gray
haze settled over the mountains; and smoke
had wormed its way into the valley, depositing a thin coating of dust on Elk Park.

Lark tackled the cleanup for a second time,
snatching up a dusty ceramic mug and
sloshing coffee across the front of her lemon-
yellow tee in the process.

Ick!

She lunged for a napkin and dabbed at the

coffee, adding a streak of raspberry jam to the stain.

Shoot. Partner or no partner, she should never have agreed to fill in for Gertie Tanager today. It wasn't part of the deal.

Nine months ago, when Esther Mills, the Warbler Café's managing partner, was murdered, Lark had agreed to handle the financial end of things — ordering, payroll, and billing. It made sense. She was the only one of the four remaining partners with any business experience.

But, she'd agreed on the condition she would never have to work the floor. Between operating the Drummond Hotel and serving as hospitality chair for the Elk Park Ornithological Chapter, Lark figured she had enough on her plate. Luckily, everyone else had concurred.

It was an arrangement that had worked well, up until today, when Cecilia called in a panic. Gertie Tanager had called in sick, no one else was available to work, and the Warbler was unseasonably busy.

Of course, by the time Lark had arrived, the rush was over.

Giving up on the raspberry-coffee collage, she pitched the napkin toward an oversized trash can standing near the wall. Another gust of wind caught the wad of paper in midair, slamming it to the deck, and tumbling it across the planking. Deck umbrellas

28

flapped and bowed. A table overturned, and cups and flatware skittered across the redwood deck.

As Lark scrambled to right the table, the *whop, whop* of a helicopter overhead shook the umbrellas. Lark glanced up and watched the helicopter churn westward until her gaze rested on the dark cloud of smoke billowing over Rocky Mountain National Park.

Lark's heart hammered in her chest. Releasing the umbrella crank, she jerked upright.

Like fog boiling onto the land, the smoke tumbled into the valley, obscuring everything in its path.

Her stomach churned. Something was wrong.

"Oh, my," said Cecilia Meyer, coming outside to join Lark at the deck railing. "You don't suppose that fire got away from them?"

"I hope not."

Until the Cerro Grande burn had roared out of control in Bandelier National Monument, Lark had never linked danger with prescribed burning. Rocky Mountain National Park conducted three burns a year. Three uneventful burns, that she would never have known took place, except for the notices printed each spring in the *Elk Park Gazette*.

But this fire was different. It had made its presence known from the git-go.

Lark had no doubts there'd be guests at

the Drummond who complained — if not about the smoke, about the noise of the helicopters, about the dust, or about the road closures in the park. Frankly, she was more worried about her friends on the fire line. Eric in particular.

Cecilia reached out an age-spotted hand and patted Lark's arm. "Now, don't you fret, dear. I'm sure he's all right."

Lark stiffened. Did she look that worried?

She scrunched her face around, trying to smooth out her brow. Her relationship with Eric was still in its fledgling stage. The last person she wanted to discuss her feelings with was Cecilia, Elk Park's self-proclaimed matchmaker.

"Honestly," continued Cecilia. "I'm sure he's just fine."

There was no point in pretending not to comprehend what she was talking about. "I'm sure they all are," said Lark, infusing her voice with a false bravado. *Think positive.*

"Just so long as no one tries playing the hero," persisted Cecilia, worrying her fingers along a seam in the tail of her blue shirt. "That's what happened to my Jimmy, you know."

For what seemed to Lark like the millionth time, Cecilia recounted the story of how forty years ago she had met and married "Jimmy" Meyer; how three days after their wedding he'd shipped out for Korea; and how several months after that, he'd been shot down under heavy fire.

"He was flying medical evac. They found the wreckage of his helicopter, but no body, so . . ." Cecilia drew a ragged breath. "They listed him missing-in-action. Just like that —" she said, snapping her fingers. "My Jimmy was gone."

Cecilia sighed, patted her shirttail into place, then stared at Lark with wet eyes the color of the hazy sky. "You know they never found him. The last time I saw Jimmy was when he waved good-bye."

Lark's thoughts flashed to the last time she'd seen Eric. He had stopped by the Drummond last night on his way home from Bird Haven. They'd sat on the porch swing, shared a cup of coffee, and talked. Banal conversation about work and sunsets and birds. As she recalled, he'd expressed some concern about the effect of today's burn on the habitat of the green-tailed towhee. But he hadn't mentioned a word about the fire danger.

He'd stayed less than an hour.

"Funny coincidence, this fire," said Cecilia, cutting into Lark's musing. "I've just been reading an article about Storm King Mountain. You remember that, don't you?"

Lark nodded. Everyone who lived in Colorado knew about the Storm King fire. Fourteen firefighters had lost their lives battling that blaze.

31

"It's a fascinating article. All about how they study fires to learn how to prevent them. The author spells out in detail everything that went wrong up on Storm King, then compares it to a fire that happened in Montana back in the forties. The Mann Gulch fire." Cecilia fluffed her mouse-brown hair, and frowned. "Funny how history repeats itself. Those two fires were nearly identical."

Lark didn't want to hear any more. "Those were wildfires, Cecilia. Both of them. This is a prescribed burn. A *controlled* burn. A burn designed to prevent catastrophic fires like those from happening."

"Is that so?" Cecilia sounded dubious. "Well, tell that to the people of Los Alamos, New Mexico."

The Cerro Grande burn. No one had died in that fire, but thousands of acres of land and hundreds of homes had been destroyed, not to mention the thousands of people who'd had to be evacuated.

Cecilia pushed back from the railing. "Oops, we have a customer."

Once her business partner had bustled away, Lark hurried to pick up the remaining dishes and throw away the rest of the trash. She *refused* to worry. Eric was a trained firefighter, among a crew of trained firefighters, and Beaver Meadows was predominately open shrub land. Everything would be okay, *unless . . .*

32

She cast a glance at the billowing smoke. *. . . the fire reached the trees.*

Bracing against another blast of wind, Lark scooped up her tray and pushed through the doors of the Warbler Café. Inside empty tables and chairs cluttered the hardwood floor, making navigation next to impossible in the dim light. Once her eyes had adjusted, she spotted Jackie Devlin, Eric's boss's wife, near the cash register.

"Can you believe all the smoke?" asked Lark, making a beeline for the kitchen.

"No," replied Cecilia and Jackie in unison.

"I hope everything's okay up there," said Lark, maneuvering her way to the counter.

Jackie shrugged, creasing her ash-blond bob. "I'm sure Wayne has everything under control. He's been concerned enough about the fire conditions for all of us. In fact, he's been out and out anal about them." She stepped forward to study the bins of coffee on display, and blocked Lark's path.

Lark stopped and repositioned the tray, balancing it against her shoulder while she waited for Jackie to move.

"At any rate," continued Jackie. "He went in early every day this week, and he left for work early again this morning. He was gone by five-thirty."

"Why?" asked Cecilia.

"Why did he leave early?" asked Jackie. "Or why was he concerned?"

33

"Both," chimed in Lark. *Talk about anal.*

"Who knows? When he left, he was mumbling something about wanting to, quote, check the humidity on Eagle Cliff Mountain, unquote. I think he was afraid it was already too dry up there, especially after this last winter." She arched a penciled eyebrow. "He must have changed his mind. After all, they lit the fire."

"I guess, but —"

"Anyway," she said, interrupting Lark and pointing to the coffee bins. "I need two pounds of *Jaltengo*. It's Wayne's favorite. And some Colombian decaf for Tamara's graduation party." She paused as though expecting a comment. "Haven't you heard? She's valedictorian of this year's senior class."

"Oh my," said Cecilia, reaching for a coffee scoop. "I didn't know. Congratulations!"

With the conversation taking a new tack, Lark grew tired of holding the tray. "Excuse me," she said.

Jackie didn't budge.

Lark tried squeezing past, clipping Jackie with the lip of the tray.

Jackie flinched, then moved aside, swatting at the back of her L.L.Bean jacket.

"Sorry," said Lark. Outside the sky had darkened, and a smokey odor permeated the room. Under her breath, she mumbled, "I still say something is wrong up there."

"Trust me," snapped Jackie. "Wayne has

been fighting fires for years. He knows what he's doing."

So did most of the guys up there. "I didn't mean anything per—"

"Though, it would have been nice if he'd waited to burn Beaver Meadows until after Tamara's party."

Was that all that bothered her? The potential impact on Tamara's big bash? No doubt the party was weeks into the planning stages. Jackie was a Martha Stewart aficionado. She even looked a little like Martha. So Jackie would be checking, rechecking, and worrying every detail until everything — right down to the cut flowers, quilted bedspreads, and clean garage — was perfect.

"I guess smoke residue does pose a problem," said Lark, pushing through the swinging doors to the kitchen. *Unbelievable.*

Depositing the tray by the sink, she leaned against the stainless steel counter, and toyed with one of her braids. There had to be a way to get some information about what was going on up there. She could try calling the firehouse. Or, better yet, she could drive up to the park.

Heading back up front to tell Cecilia she was leaving, Lark scooped up a handful of chocolate-covered coffee beans and caught sight of her reflection in the bottom of a Revere Ware skillet. Shoots of hair sprouted from her blond braids. A streak of soot marked her nose. *Heidi meets Pippi Long-stocking.* No wonder Jackie had shied away.

As Lark wiped the soot off her nose, Cecilia's voice drifted back toward the kitchen. "So, Jackie, how *is* Wayne? He came in a few days ago, and —"

"Fine." The word blared from Jackie's mouth on a high note, and Lark nearly choked on her candy.

What was Cecilia thinking? Granted, Wayne's odd behavior was the talk of the town. Only last week he'd wandered into the Warbler, sat down, and stared at the menu board for a full ten minutes. He'd left without speaking to anyone and without ordering a thing. But, even so, asking Jackie about it was like treading on tundra.

"He's fine," Jackie repeated an octave lower.

Lark emerged from the kitchen.

"Really?" said Cecilia. "I thought he acted rather strange the last time I saw him."

Jackie's face froze, and she gestured toward the coffee bin. "Haven't you got better things to do than gossip about your customers?"

"Oh my. I didn't mean —"

"No," Jackie interrupted. "You didn't *think.*"

It was time to intervene.

Lark stepped forward. Prying the half-filled coffee bag from Cecilia's hand, she shooed her toward the kitchen, hoping to avoid a showdown. When Cecilia had moved out of earshot, Lark turned to Jackie. "She didn't mean anything negative. She's just concerned about Wayne. We all are."

"Take my word for it, he's fine."

Rather than pressing the issue or continuing to apologize, Lark dropped the subject and shoveled another scoop of coffee beans into the bag she'd taken from Cecilia. After filling a second bag, she set them both on the counter. "Four pounds. Do you need anything else?"

Jackie shook her head.

Lark punched in the amounts on the cash register and hit the enter key. The drawer dinged open. The fire siren blared.

Chapter 4

Within minutes, the fire had crowned in the ponderosa. Eric searched the crowd for Nora Frank, skimming the worried faces of the firefighters through his binoculars. He didn't spot her.

"Linenger?" Pacey Trent's voice crackled through the radio. Up to this point, the Intermountain Regional FMO had been screaming for Nora.

Eric unhooked the handheld from his belt. *"Ja?"*

"Have you seen your boss?"

"No." Eric hated the sinking sensation gnawing at the pit of his stomach. Nora should have picked up the summons. Radio range in Colorado was limited only by miles or mountains. Neither reason was applicable, based on where she should be.

"Where the f—" Static deleted the expletive, and when Trent's voice returned, he was saying, "— evacuate the Visitor Center."

The Intermountain Regional FMO wheezed, then coughed. He must be eating smoke, thought Eric.

"Then get on the horn," continued Trent, "and get people up there to evacuate that housing development on the east end of Beaver Meadows, the Wildland Center, and the Youth Mountain."

"How much time do we have?"

Static hissed across the band. The radio sputtered and popped. Finally Trent answered. "I thought we'd backed her down, but she's on a run. At this rate, we'll have fire at the Visitor Center in under an hour."

"I'm on it, sir." Eric didn't wait for a response. He switched frequencies and radioed dispatch. "We need to evacuate all locations along Highway 66."

Within minutes, the dispatcher on duty radioed back to let him know she'd talked to Dorothy MacBean at the Wildland Center and Vic Garcia, the Elk Park County sheriff. "Vic's already up at the Youth Mountain Camp," she said. "But, FYI, all I get at the housing development is Gene Paxton's voice mail."

Five minutes later, Eric put one wheel in the ditch and jounced his truck around Bernie Crandall's empty squad car. It was pulled crosswise in the road, preventing travel up U.S. 36 — a precaution Nora had instituted when the fire first bolted on them. Fairly effective, when manned. So where the heck was Bernie?

Eric wheeled into the parking lot, keeping one eye out for Elk Park's police chief, and one eye on the milling throng. The parking lot was jammed full of cars, and people.

The press had pitched camp at the western-most end, setting up tripods with cameras near the rear of their trucks. Shutters clicked as occasional spurts of fire erupted above the tree line. Video cameras whirred. News anchors jabbered into microphones and gestured wildly toward the park and the mushrooming cloud.

Eric downshifted. Inching his way through the vehicles and people, he wondered if Linda Verbiscar was among the crowd.

Not likely. Over an hour ago, she and her cameraman had headed around to where the crews were building the fire line. Most likely, the two KEPC-TV employees had come down past the Visitor Center and headed up Highway 66 — the next route on the evacuation trail.

Anyway, Eric didn't have time to worry about them now. If they reached the fire line, Trent would take care of them.

A tourist stood in the road, snapping pictures with a disposable camera. Eric swerved to avoid hitting him, tromping on the brakes and swinging his truck into a "No Parking" zone near the building. Maybe Bernie would show up to give him a ticket, and Eric could put him to work clearing the parking lot.

The Visitor Center overlooked the east end of Beaver Meadows. Built of stone and mortar, it was listed on the National Register of Historic Places and housed Park Service offices, a theater, bookstore, public bathrooms, and a mini-museum.

Eric skirted the edge of the self-guided nature trail and banged through the wooden doors. Bernie Crandall leaned against a glass-covered counter, flirting with the seasonal park ranger on duty.

Neither one glanced up. The ranger giggled at something Bernie said and pointed to a spot on one of the three-dimensional topography maps — designed more to impress the millions of visitors that passed through Rocky Mountain National Park each year, than for the actual convenience of the park rangers. Bernie feigned interest.

"Hey, what's with the abandoned police car on the road out there?" asked Eric, announcing his presence.

A tourist at the next counter glanced up. Eric ignored him, and the tourist ambled away.

"Yo, Linenger," said Bernie, straightening up and offering his hand. "I had to use the facilities and got distracted by this lovely Smokey Bearess." He winked at the girl, and she giggled again. "I was just heading out."

"Great," said Eric, returning the shake. "Because we need to clear the building and the parking lot, now."

The police chief sobered. "What's up?"

"The fire jumped the line to the southeast, and it's spreading. It's in the trees on Eagle Cliff."

Bernie let out a low whistle. "How much time did they give us?"

"Give or take? About twenty minutes."

A gust of wind rattled the Visitor Center's windows. Bernie donned his "I'm in charge" manner and broke for the door. "Okay, here's what we're going to do," he ordered. "You run a sweep in here, and I'll clear the parking lot."

The door banged shut behind him, and Eric turned to the young ranger. She looked fresh out of acne, and plenty scared.

"Do you have any idea how many people are in the building?" he asked.

The girl shook her head, swishing her ponytail from side to side. "A couple of rangers, and a few tourists, maybe. But . . ." Embarrassed, she glanced away. "I wasn't paying a lot of attention."

"Don't worry about it . . ." He strained to read her name tag. "Susie?"

She nodded.

"Great, Susie. Let's start with the other rangers?"

"Someone's always in the bookstore. And I imagine there's still somebody in the office. Everyone else went to check on the fire."

That made sense to Eric. It's where he would have been.

"No problem. But what we need to do is get everyone out of the building. Everyone. No one should be left behind. Got that?"

"Yeah." She sounded hesitant.

"As soon as the building's clear, we'll lock it up tight."

Red splotches bloomed on the girl's face. She nodded, blinking rapidly.

Don't lose it on me now, Ranger.

"Check the upstairs," he ordered. "Search the back offices, the ladies' room, the book-store . . . anywhere someone might be. I'll cover the downstairs and meet you back here in five minutes."

He started to step away, but Susie's arm darted out, and she grabbed hold of his sleeve. "Are we in any danger?"

Did he hear a tremble in her voice?

"I don't think so," he said, trying to sound reassuring. In truth, the fire was too close for comfort. "With any luck, it'll sweep south." He glanced out the window toward Beaver Meadows, but couldn't see the fire through the trees.

Susie relaxed her grip.

"You okay?" he asked.

The girl nodded.

"Then let's get started."

Susie sprinted toward the offices, and Eric headed downstairs. He rattled the doors of the walk-out basement, then moved to the auditorium where voices spilled from behind the curtain. Yanking it open, he found a small group of people engrossed in watching the endless tape of rangers answering questions about the park. Eric cut the power to the projector. The image flickered to black.

"Sorry folks. I'm afraid I have to ask you to leave."

He fielded a volley of questions, then marshaled them to the stairs. Making a pit stop to clear out the men's room, he followed them up to the main floor and found Susie waiting for him.

"Do we have everyone?"

She nodded, then handed him the keys. By the time he finished locking the doors, Bernie had cleared the parking lot.

Without the chatter of people, the fire's growl was audible in the distance. Smoke eddied through the treetops, casting a pall on the landscape. Wind roared in the branches, and wildlife skittered in all directions. Not a single bird sang. Only the shrill call of a raven echoed across the land.

Eric, Bernie, and Susie huddled on the sidewalk. Eric shouted to be heard above the wind. "I sent the check-point ranger to seal off traffic at Marys Lake Road. We need to get him some help."

Bernie nodded.

"We need to clear that road to Highway 7, plus clear Highway 66 and Bear Lake Road."

Bernie flashed a thumbs-up. "I've already

got dispatch rounding up all the reserve officers."

Eric nodded, then turned to Susie. "I want
you to take your truck down to the west end
of town. Set up a roadblock. Don't let
anyone except fire or emergency personnel
pass," he ordered. "Understand?"

She didn't respond.

Small fires glowed through the gaps in the
trees, and ash sprinkled around them like
snow. Eric gripped the girl's shoulders, snapping her out of her daze. "Repeat what I
said," he demanded.

"Only fire and emergency personnel." Her
voice sounded flat.

"Good. Now, go." As she scampered away,
he turned to Bernie. "We need to post an officer with her."

"Sure thing." Bernie rubbed his chin as
though testing his shave.

Eric shook his head in disgust. "She's a
kid, Bernie."

"She's gotta be eighteen."

"And you're what? My age?"

Bernie had to be at least thirty-five,
thought Eric. Nearly old enough to be the
girl's father. What the hell was Bernie
thinking?

"Youth has its advantages."

"You're a sick man," said Eric. "But, hey,
since you like kids so much, I'm sure Vic
needs a hand evacuating the Youth Mountain

45

Camp. I don't know how many adults they have up there, but it can't be enough."

The Youth Mountain Camp housed up to one hundred fifty troubled teenagers. This time of year it would be chock full. No picnic for the counselors, even on a good day.

"Gotcha," said Bernie. "Let me get my men situated, and I'll catch up to you there." He lit out for his squad car, then looked back around. "I take it that's where you're headed?"

Eric nodded his head. "But I've got two stops to make first. One at the Wildland Center, and one at Shangri-la."

The Wildland Center was locked up tight by the time Eric arrived. Dorothy MacBean and Forest Nettleman must have wasted no time in clearing out the tourists and heading into town. Dorothy was probably holed up at the Warbler Café by now, recounting the terrible danger to Lark and Cecilia.

He figured Lark was worried about the fire by now. As soon as he had a chance, he'd call.

In contrast to the Wildland Center, Shangri-la bustled with activity.

Named for an imaginary paradise on earth, the housing development squatted two miles off of Highway 66, on the backside of Eagle Cliff Mountain. A large sign marked the entrance. It read, "Buy a Slice of Utopia."

Beyond the open gate, a pock-marked gravel road wound uphill, dead-ending near a scattered group of slab foundations. Once part of a homestead, the original property had been parceled and bought, parceled and bought, and subsequently parceled into eighty thirty-five-acre building lots. The planned homes sold in the eight hundred thousand dollar-plus range, but only two had been finished. In most cases, wells had been dug, septic systems laid, foundations poured, and a smattering of sites had seen some degree of framing.

Today, workers crawled over the roofs of the two roughed-in houses. The bang of nail-guns vibrated the air in defiance of the wind. Eric doubted the workers had planned on it either.

A sagging, double-wide trailer marked "Office" stood guard where the gravel ended. Stacks of lumber surrounded the building on three sides, and a red all terrain vehicle was parked on the other. Overturned buckets, white paint dripping down the sides, blocked access to the Dumpster.

Eric parked his pickup in front and charged up the steps. As he ducked through the doorway, Mandy Hathaway, the developer's secretary, glanced up from her book.

"Is your boss in?" he asked.

"Nope," she replied, tucking a long strand

of dark hair behind her ear.

"Do you know where he is?"

"Nope."

A veritable fountain of information. "Well, do you know if he's somewhere on site?"

Tossing her reading glasses onto the desk, she rubbed her eyes, making him wait for an answer. Finally, she said, "He was around a couple of hours ago. I haven't seen him in a while." She jutted out her chin. "Want me to give him a message?"

Eric wondered if this was her way of running interference for Gene Paxton. Rumors were flying that he was in financial trouble, hocked up to his eyeballs to some "good old boys" in New Jersey.

"Look, I don't have time for this," said Eric. The last radio contact with Trent placed the fire within two miles of Shangri-la. Unless they hurried, the road back to town would be impassable, stranding them all in the path of the fire. "Here's the deal. We have a fire burning in the park."

"I know," she blurted out. "Ben's up there."

Suddenly she frowned and leaned forward. Thin-boned hands clicked the stems of her glasses together. "Everything's okay, isn't it?"

Damn. He'd forgotten Ben Hathaway served on the volunteer fire department.

"Everyone's fine," said Eric, raising his hands to stop her from drawing conclusions.

"But the fire got away from us. We need to evacuate."

He watched her closely, making sure his words sunk in, then he pointed toward the finished houses. "Are people living there?"

Mandy sprang into action, riffling through the files in her desk drawer. "The owners of 303 haven't occupied yet, but the Larsons live in 305. I can give them a call."

"What about the workers?"

"Gene always goes up there in person. As far as I know, those guys don't have a radio. Or a cell phone. Even if they did, I don't have the number." She yanked a manila file out of the drawer. "Give me a sec, and I'll try and reach him on his cell phone."

Gravel crunched in front of the trailer, and Eric glanced out the window. "No need," he said. "Paxton just pulled in."

Eric watched as Gene Paxton jammed the gearshift into park and clambered out of the pickup. Five years younger than Eric, he lumbered like an old man. Short and stout, beard tinged gray, his belly protruded out over his belt. Instinctively, Eric sucked in his gut.

With a sideways glance at the Park Service truck, Paxton tossed something into the tool carrier mounted in the bed of his pickup, dusted his jeans with his baseball cap, and ambled toward the steps. "Hey ya, Ranger. How ya doin'?" he asked, exaggerating an already thick accent, and sounding like Joey from *Friends*. "To what do we owe the pleasure?"

Eric told him about the evacuation order.

"Geez." Gene rubbed his balding head. "I thought it looked like a lot of smoke. So, what are you saying? Are you thinkin' Shangri-la's gonna burn to the ground?"

"No," said Eric, not anxious to be misquoted for a second time today. "All I can say is, the fire's headed this way and an evacuation has been ordered. The Park Service and U.S. Forest Service are working on controlling the fire. We hope to have it contained soon. We just can't take any chances." Eric moved toward the door. "Grab what you need, but do it quickly. You have about ten minutes, then you and Mandy need to head into town."

"What about the office? I can't leave my files, and all my records."

"Ten minutes," repeated Eric. "Take what's most important. Leave the rest."

It differed with everyone. More than once Eric had contemplated what he would save if he were about to lose everything to the fire. The animals were a given. After that, he would save the picture of his father.

He drove up the hill, stopping at the first house. Two stories up, roofers drove nails into asphalt shingles, the sun transforming their bodies to silhouettes against the deep blue sky.

A compressor hissed, then recharged. A radio blared. Eric shouted, waving his arms.

Nothing.

Unable to draw a response, he climbed the ladder, scrambling to the peak of the roof. "Hello?"

The nearest worker jerked his head up. An asphalt shingle tore free of his grip. Both men watched as the wind carried the shingle high in the air, twisting it, turning it, before slamming it to the ground.

"Whew," whistled the roofer.

Eric nodded, then pointed toward the smoke billowing up from the park. "You guys need to pack it up."

The roofer frowned. *"Lo siento, pero no le he entendido."*

What had he said? *Lo siento* meant sorry in Spanish. But what did the rest mean?

The roofer tried again. *"No comprendo."*

"Ja." He didn't understand. "You wouldn't by any chance speak Norwegian?"

The roofer cocked his head.

"I didn't think so." Eric tried taking a different tack and pantomimed putting away tools. "You need to stop working, and leave."

The man shrugged and looked back at his coworkers.

"You need to *go*," said Eric. He pointed toward the road. Pretending to pick up the tools, he strutted along the roof.

The roofers chuckled.

"Great," said Eric. "Does anyone speak English?"

One kid stepped forward. "Yes, I speak a little."

"Good." Eric signaled him to come closer. "Can you explain to your foreman that you have to leave? You are in danger here." He pointed toward the smoke. A helicopter dragging a bucket dumped water on the fire. Eric watched it swing back toward the lake, then his gaze shifted left. His heart banged in his chest.

Damn.

Uphill of the main fire and closer to them, a separate column of smoke twisted into the air.

Chapter 5

A spot fire! How the hell had he missed it?

Eric raised his binoculars and grabbed for the radio. "Butch. Trent. Do you copy?"

"Yeah." Butch Hanley's voice scratched across the band.

"We have a spot fire to the south on Eagle Cliff Mountain, over."

The radio hissed. Finally, Butch said, "I don't see it."

"It could be hidden behind the spur from you." Eric made a sweep with his binoculars. The fire was tucked into a draw. From most angles its plume would be masked by the smoke from the burn. "It's fair-sized. I'd say it's been burning awhile."

"Is it threatening property?" asked Trent, joining the conversation.

Eric knew he meant buildings. "No, but —"

"Then continue with the e-vac," ordered Trent. "After that's complete, you can check out the spot and report back."

Eric's hands tightened around his binoculars. Trent was right. Standard policy required that public safety, and the safety of the firefighters, come before the preservation of property, or, in this case, forest. Eric's assignment was to ensure no one was trapped by fire south of the junction of Highway 66 and U.S. 36.

Shooing the workers off the roof, he scrambled down the ladder and moved on to the next house. Precious minutes ticked by. The ten he'd given Paxton stretched to twenty. Finally, after nearly half an hour, the last person was herded out of the subdivision and Gene Paxton locked the gate to Shangri-la.

When Paxton's truck disappeared to the north, Eric turned south onto Highway 66 toward the Youth Mountain Camp. The road wound through a canyon, alongside the Wind River. Eagle Cliff Mountain rose to the west, Gianttrack Mountain to the east.

Eric tapped his brakes and slowed the truck to a crawl. Keeping one hand on the wheel and one eye on the road, he peered through the truck's passenger window at the craggy backside of Eagle Cliff Mountain. He didn't like what he saw.

In the first place, the configuration of mountains, road, and river created a natural wind tunnel. Air currents drifted lazily into the canyon, only to pick up speed and funnel out the gulches, etched like fingers into the mountainside.

In the second place, the terrain was steep and clogged with vegetation. Down nearer the road, the grade rose gradually covered in clusters of yellow monkeyflower, quivering aspen, and the occasional pine. But several hundred yards uphill, the gentle slopes pitched, weaving together a tangled mass of understory. The terrain rose sharply in elevation, plateaued, then climbed again.

The worst part was, somewhere up there a fire burned out of control.

Jackie Devlin had told him Wayne left early to check out the humidity on Eagle Cliff Mountain. Was he up there somewhere? Maybe trapped by the fire?

Movement in the trees caught Eric's attention. A red-naped sapsucker drilled orderly holes in the bark of a pine, while swallows flitted in and out of the aspens. Nesting pairs.

He watched the birds for a moment, then focused on finding the spot fire. If his perspective from the roof at Shangri-la had been correct, it was over one spur from Hanley's crew. Which meant, *after* he finished helping Vic evacuate the Youth Mountain Camp, his best bet in locating the fire was to hike in up the first gully, past the woodpecker.

The Youth Mountain Camp was situated at the end of Highway 66. An old YMCA camp, it was composed of a main lodge surrounded in semicircle formation by six large dormitory cabins. Four of the cabins housed boys, and two of the cabins housed girls. Each cabin held twenty-five kids and two counselors.

Vic Garcia, the Elk Park County sheriff, lived in the main lodge. After his girlfriend and Lark's partner, Esther Mills, was murdered, Vic had petitioned the board of directors of the Youth Mountain Camp to let him renovate the third floor offices into a caretaker's apartment. The directors quickly agreed. Given the criminal history of the campers, having the sheriff on site was a definite plus.

Eric figured it meant the evacuation of the campers would be well under way.

To his surprise, when he pulled up in front of the lodge, he found two empty Elk Park County School District buses parked at the curb. Kids swarmed the grassy area around the flagpole and clustered around Bernie's squad car, parked diagonally at the curb with its lights still flashing.

"Over here, Linenger," Bernie shouted, waving a clipboard high in the air. Big, blond, and beefy, he was hard to miss. Next to him, Vic Garcia — short, dark-skinned, and fifty-something — blended in with the crowd.

Eric sprinted toward them.

"We were just about to start loading the buses," said Bernie. "We're short drivers, so I could only snag two from the high school. We're going to have to cart some of the kids down in YMC vans."

Vic nodded. "Hello, Eric."

"Vic."

"The Red Cross is setting up cots at the school," he said. "Once we load the kids up, we'll head down there and feed them some lunch."

"Sounds like a good plan," said Eric. "But we need to get moving."

Loading up this many kids was going to take a while.

"We're just waiting on my men to finish sweeping the dorm areas," explained Bernie. "We want to make damn sure no one is left behind when we roll."

"Another good idea," said Eric. "But we can't wait any longer. We need to start loading the buses now."

For someone raised in fire country, Bernie didn't seem to be grasping the urgency of the situation.

Vic hitched up his pants at the waistband. "That's what I said. I suggested we put them on the buses and check off their names against the camp roster. That way we'd know for sure we have everyone, and we'd be ready to go when the sweep was done."

Bernie tensed. This was his jurisdiction. The Youth Mountain Camp was on city-owned property, so Bernie called the shots.

Too bad. "Vic's right," said Eric.

"You guys want to do it that way? Be my guest." Bernie slapped the clipboard against the flat of Vic's stomach. "Go for it."

Vic grabbed the clipboard. He stiffened,

absorbing the blow.

Eric sucked in air and waited for the sparks to fly. It was no secret the two men disliked each other. Vic had never forgiven Bernie for treating him like a suspect in Esther's murder, and Bernie begrudged the sheriff his power.

Vic stroked his mustache, then signaled to one of the staff members. The counselor blew a whistle, and teenagers froze in place. A Frisbee clattered to the sidewalk. Britney Spears's voice blared from a boom box, and one of the hip-hop dancers scrambled to turn it off.

"Okay, listen up!" hollered Vic. "When you hear your name, I want you to step forward. We're going to check your name off the list, and you're going to get on a bus. Grab your gear."

Some of the kids complied, snatching up duffel bags and moving toward the sidewalk. Others remained where they were. One girl wept on the steps of the lodge, while a boy tried comforting her.

"Acevedo, Joseph!" yelled a counselor.

A scrawny young man with limp black hair stepped forward. His name was checked off, and he boarded the first bus.

"Anderson, George."

"Atencio, Leon."

Names were called off, and one by one the kids boarded the buses in orderly fashion.

"Kennedy, Lewis, the third."

No one stepped forward.

Eric looked at Vic.

"He's a new kid," explained the sheriff. "A problem. Comes from a wealthy family. His nickname is Tres, pronounced 'tray,' French for third."

"Does anyone know where Kennedy is?" bellowed Bernie from the other side of the flagpole. A few of the kids started fidgeting.

A reflex reaction to trouble, or did one of them know something?

Bernie must have noticed, too, because he pointed a finger at one of the boys. "*You*, step forward."

The kid raised a defiant chin. "I don't know nothing."

"Anything," corrected Vic, hightailing it across the grass. He stepped in between the boy and Bernie. "Are you sure?"

The boy looked down. "Last I seen him, he was with Justin."

"Justin Suett?"

The boy nodded.

Eric moved in closer.

"Suett, Justin!" hollered Bernie in a Marine sergeant voice.

No response.

"Another problem," Vic muttered under his breath.

Did he mean Suett, or Bernie?

"Where did you last see them?" demanded Bernie.

Again the kid raised his chin.

"It's important," said Vic.

The boy narrowed his eyes. Ignoring Bernie, he met Vic's gaze. "They was headed out the back of the dorm."

"What time?" Bernie asked.

The kid puffed out a breath and kicked at the grass edging the sidewalk. "Geez, man. How am I supposed to know? It was early, okay?"

"How early?"

"It was still dark."

Vic put the boy on the bus, while Bernie and his deputies conducted a search of the boys' rooms in the Kokopeli Dorm. By the time Eric and Vic got to the room, they had turned up nothing. No Tres. No Justin. No belongings. And no indication of where the boys might have gone.

"Damn, just what we need," said Bernie, flopping down on one of the bunks in Tres's room. "Two missing persons."

"Three," corrected Eric. He told them about Wayne Devlin not showing up for work this morning. Then Nora Frank's disappearance flashed through his mind. Maybe they should up the count to four.

"Yeah, well, we all know Devlin's been acting a little strange lately. Hell, for all you know, he might have forgotten about the burn and gone fishing." Bernie beat a rhythm on the bed railing. "But these two boys disappearing . . . this is a serious matter."

Eric bristled. Didn't anyone else care that Wayne Devlin hadn't been seen since five-thirty this morning? That was over six hours ago.

"Where would the boys have headed?" asked Bernie.

Vic crossed his arms, puffing air from between his lips. "Let's see. They most likely lit out for Denver. Tres's folks live in the Cherry Creek area. Justin's live out in Castle Pines. They're both pretty spoiled kids, so I doubt either one of them would try and go very far without some money in their pockets. My guess is they headed home."

"Is that where most of your escapees head?" goaded Bernie.

Vic's eyes narrowed. "It doesn't happen very often."

Eric's gaze traveled between the two men. "Would they have taken the road?"

"Possibly," Vic said.

Eric hadn't seen anyone hitchhiking. He walked over to the window and glanced up at the mountain. Smoke boiled over the ridge.

He tapped on the pane. "We need to keep moving."

A moment passed, then Bernie turned to one of his deputies. "Have them finish loading the buses."

"Thanks," said Eric after the deputy hustled away. Once the kids were loaded up and headed toward town, his responsibilities to the e-vac operation ended. The missing kids were Bernie and Vic's problem.

"What are we going to do about them?" asked Vic, nodding to a picture of Tres and Justin thumbtacked to the bulletin board near the window. "The one on the left is Tres."

Eric studied the photograph. It was taken in front of the lodge. Lewis Kennedy the third, Tres, had his arm draped around Justin Suett's shoulder.

Tres was a scrawny, scruffy-looking teenager with a bad case of acne. Taller than Justin Suett by a head, his lip bore the trace of a blond mustache. He stared out of the picture with blue eyes the color of faded denim.

Justin looked clean-cut by comparison. Stocky, with close-cropped brown hair, an easy smile, and dark eyes, he looked like the kid next door. The type of boy mothers loved their girls to bring home. Eric wondered what they'd done to end up here.

"I'll put out an APB," said Bernie. "And then we hope —"

"Sir!" A young officer dashed into the room, cradling his hat like a football. "We have a problem, sir."

Bernie raked a hand through his hair. "What is it now? Not another missing kid?"

"No, sir. We found some tracks, sir."

"Tracks?"

Vic and Bernie headed for the door. Eric followed. Outside, smoke poured over the top of the ridge, and a dusting of ash sprinkled from the sky. Eric felt a sudden panic. They'd waited too long to evacuate.

"We need to get the rest of these kids out of here, now," he said.

Bernie held up a beefy finger. "Where do the tracks lead?"

"Into the woods, sir. The boys headed into the woods."

Chapter 6

The shriek of the fire siren unnerved Lark, sending a series of shivers along her arms and curling the hairs along her neck. The wail could only mean one thing. The burn was out of control.

Lark looked toward the window. The sky had darkened appreciably, smoke blotting out the sunshine, and large flakes of ash lashed the windows, reminiscent of a late-spring snow.

Slamming the cash register drawer shut, she shoved a handful of coins into Jackie's cupped hand. "Here's your change."

"Oh my." Cecilia emerged from the kitchen wiping her hands on a dish towel. "How bad do you suppose —"

Lark cut her off by snatching up the phone and dialing the firehouse.

A small town measured its heart through its volunteers. And, despite its transient nature, Elk Park had a big heart. Excluding the paid fire chief and a handful of paramedics, Elk Park County's Fire Department was a one hundred percent volunteer operation with one-third of Elk Park's households represented. Fire was a major threat along the front range. Those who were able served. Those who weren't provided backup services.

Lark had signed on the year she bought the Drummond Hotel. Since surviving the training, she'd fought several house fires caused by someone leaving a stove on or a cigarette burning, several restaurant fires caused by grease, worked hand line on the Bobcat forest fire, and assisted Mountain Search and Rescue in finding numerous lost tourists in the park.

The phone was answered on the second ring. "Fire dispatch."

"This is Lark Drummond."

"They're asking all available volunteer personnel to report to Prospect Point for briefing."

"I'm on my way." Lark hung up the phone and reached for her jacket, rooting in her pocket for her truck keys. "They want everyone," she explained.

A bad sign. Usually after a call went out, a number sufficient to man the equipment showed up, and the remaining volunteers were put on standby.

Cecilia laid the dish towel on the counter. "Promise me you'll be careful."

Jackie furrowed her brow. "Why Prospect Point? I thought the burn was in Beaver Meadows."

"*Was* being the operative word." Lark

hugged Cecilia. "Try not to worry. I'll call you as soon as I'm back."

Peeling out of the parking lot, Lark headed to the Drummond to pick up her fire gear. No sooner had she pulled up in front of the carriage house, than Stephen Velof, the Drummond's manager, marched across the parking lot to her door.

"Lark, we have a problem."

"We always have a problem, Stephen. Right now, I'm in a hurry." She tapped her ear and pointed at the air. The siren still blared.

"That's the problem. Some of the guests are worried. A few have checked out early, and several are demanding refunds for previous nights' stays." His clipped words fit his stiff persona. Velof's blond hair rose in a fuzz of small, fashionable spikes. Piercing blue eyes peered out above a hawkish nose.

"Stephen, if people want to leave, let them. As for giving them their money back, you decide what's fair." She bounded up the steps of the front porch.

Velof dogged her heels. "No refund is fair. It isn't our fault they can't get into the park. It's an act of God."

"Or the Park Service."

"Right." Velof held the screen while she opened the door. Stepping into the kitchen, she tossed her keys on the counter where they'd be easy to find, and headed for the bedroom.

"Consider it a goodwill gesture, Stephen. Offer a discount."

"And suffer the negative impact to pre-season sales figures?" Velof marched behind her, as she threaded her way through the living room and down the hall.

"Perhaps the bigger concern is June," she said, giving him something more to worry about. Once word of the fire spread, they were bound to see cancellations.

Velof sniffed. "You're right. I hadn't thought of that. We should institute a public relations campaign immediately. We can make flyers."

"You do that." Lark spun around, blocking the entrance to her bedroom. "I need to change."

"Oh." His face pinked. "Sorry."

As he backed away, Lark swung the door shut in his face. "I hired you because I trusted you to make decisions," she called through the door, stripping off her shorts. "So go forth and manage."

"I am trying to share my concerns with you," Velof whined. "Don't you find it disconcerting that people are leaving?"

"Frankly, at the moment, I'm more worried about the fire." If it roared through town, it could wipe out everything she owned, all that she'd worked so hard to build over the past three years. Every last dime she had was invested in the Drummond and the Warbler.

Her existence hinged on her habitat, not on a couple of months worth of revenue.

She stripped off her stained T-shirt and dropped it on the floor. After yanking a clean one out of her drawer, she snatched her fire clothes off a hook in the back of her closet. The outfit — made of standard issue Nomex, a fire-resistant material that allowed for little ventilation — would be bulky and hot, so she swiped on additional deodorant. Useless against the heat of a fire, but at least she wouldn't smell rank before everyone else did.

After donning the clean T-shirt, she pulled on the yellow Nomex shirt, then the green Nomex pants with the yellow suspenders. Grabbing a pair of wool socks, she headed back for the kitchen.

Velof, who was still leaning against the wall, followed her back down the hall. "Where are you going?"

"Where does it look like I'm going?" Lark grabbed her fire boots from behind the kitchen door and flopped down in a chair to pull on her socks.

"You're not headed up to the fire."

"Yes, that's exactly where I'm going, Stephen." Jamming her feet into her boots, she laced them quickly, then pulled her pant legs down over the tops and grabbed her fire pack off the peg beside the door.

Out of habit, she checked the contents. Last time she'd gone out on a fire, she'd grabbed her birdwatching pack and ended up with a field guide, small notebook, pen, sunscreen, lip balm, water bottle, granola bar, penknife, and binoculars. In contrast, the fire pack contained a hard hat, goggles, knife, fire shelter, gloves, snacks, water, and an extra T-shirt. Everything else she needed by way of equipment, the Fire Department or Park Service would supply.

Slinging the pack over her shoulder, she headed out. Velof held open the door.

"You're still here?" Lark asked, knowing perfectly well he hadn't left.

He dutifully ignored her. "I can't believe you're going off to fight fires. You have enough to put out right here. You're a hotel proprietor for God's sake."

"I'm also a volunteer fireman." She bullied her way past him, leaping down the stairs two at a time.

"When will you be back?" he asked, his voice striking a plaintive note.

"I don't know. When the fire's out." She pitched her backpack into the cab of the pickup. "Meanwhile, just make a decision." *That's what you're being paid for.* "Trust your instincts, Stephen. That's what I try and do."

Lark left Velof standing on the front porch and drove her pickup through town. Ash rained down, coating the windshield. She flipped on her wipers. The ash was not a good sign, but it didn't necessarily mean the fire was headed their direction. Depending on the wind, ash could carry for miles.

Along the streets, tourists huddled under the eaves of the buildings, some staring incredulously at the sky, others peering into the shops that lined Main Street. Many of the stores were closed. Several sported "Gone to Fire" signs in the window.

Turning left at the intersection, she accelerated up U.S. 36. The stores and people dropped away, replaced by scattered houses tucked among the trees. Elk grazed like horses on the front lawns. Bluebirds flitted from fence post to fence post.

The first sign of trouble came as she rounded the bend onto the straightaway that led to the park. A National Park Service truck blocked the westbound lane, guarded by a young ranger. The ranger stepped forward and raised her hand.

Lark braked and rolled to a stop, lowering her window.

"You need to turn around, ma'am," said the ranger, a young girl in an oversized hat covered in soot. "The park is closed to all traffic."

Since when had she become a "ma'am"? In her mind's eye she wasn't much older than the ranger. "I'm a volunteer firefighter," Lark explained.

The ranger eyed her skeptically. "I don't see any emergency markings on your vehicle, ma'am, and I'm under strict orders not to let anyone through except official emergency personnel."

Lark glanced down at her attire. What, did she look like she was on her way to a birdwatching convention?

Rather than say something flip, she tried reasoning with the girl. "I'm wearing fire gear. I have my pack." She gestured toward the seat beside her. "What more proof do you need?"

"I need to see some credentials, ma'am. Do you have a badge?"

"No," answered Lark. Though, come to think of it, they'd given her a card when she passed her training. She didn't know she was supposed to carry it. No one had ever asked to see it before.

"Do you have anything proving you're a firefighter?"

"Aside from the clothes?" asked Lark. The girl was starting to get on her nerves. "No. But why else would I dress like this?"

"I don't know, ma'am. Perhaps to gain access to a restricted area."

Vehicles started stacking up behind the pickup. A few sported the red flashing emergency lights designated for volunteers, but most ran bare. A horn blared. Susie eyed them nervously, but stood her ground.

"I'm sorry," she said. "But I can't let you through. That's what they told me. Only offi-

71

cial emergency personnel."

"Look, Ranger . . ." Lark grappled for words, unsure how to reason with someone so young and determined. "Susie. There isn't time for this. I *am* official emergency personnel. The sirens went off, I called in, and was told to report to Prospect Point. We all were." Lark jerked a thumb toward the line of cars behind her. "Now you can either let me pass, or I'm going to run your roadblock."

The girl stepped back, then moved in front of Lark's truck, placing her palms on the hood. "I'm sorry. I can't let you do that, ma'am."

The absurdity of the situation struck Lark as funny, and she struggled not to laugh. "Get out of the way," she ordered.

"No." The girl planted her feet a foot apart, hands on her hips, lips set in a hard line.

"Then at least stop calling me ma'am."

That drew a smile.

Encouraged, Lark pushed open the door and climbed out of the truck. The ash pelted her head and slicked the asphalt. "Use your head, Susie. Why else would we all be up here? Sure, one of us might be bluffing. But all of us?" She held her hands wide, palms up, and shook them toward the lineup of vehicles.

A horn blast punctuated Lark's point.

More horns blared. Several cars pulled forward using the eastbound lanes. The ranger backed up to straddle the gap between her truck and the ditch.

Harry Eckles, a volunteer fireman who taught biology at the University of Colorado in Boulder, inched his red compact up alongside Lark's truck. She knew him best through his association with the Elk Park Ornithological Chapter. He'd been an EPOCH member for years. Sandy-haired, muscular, with blue eyes, which he covered only when wearing his reading glasses, she'd found him attractive at first. It had taken her six months of flirting to figure out he was gay.

"What's the holdup?" he asked, craning to see Lark out the passenger window.

She leaned down, crossing her arms on the sill. "We're not official enough." Lark recapped the conversation with Susie.

"She's telling you the truth," Harry called to the ranger.

"Unless you can prove you're a fireman, I cannot let you pass," said Susie, bottom lip quivering. Determination, or fear? Her eyes widened when one of the drivers behind Harry revved his engine. "Please, don't."

Watching Susie, hearing the fear in her voice, caused Lark's anger to evaporate. She suddenly remembered she'd once been in a similar position.

Years ago, when she was a college freshman

home on vacation, Lark's father — the senior senator from Connecticut — had come under scrutiny for having an alleged affair with a campaign worker. Her mother, at her father's urging, had thrown a party for some two hundred of their closest friends in order to quash the rumors. Lark had been charged with checking the invitations at the door in order to keep out the press.

Things had gone fine, until one very good-looking young man without an invitation, and claiming to be the aide to the senator from Delaware, cajoled her into letting him pass. He'd turned out to be a *Washington Post* reporter. Her father had never forgotten.

Lark shook off the memory. "Who gave you your orders?"

A pained expression crossed Susie's face. "I know this is going to sound dumb, but I don't remember his name."

She was right. It sounded ludicrous.

"Do you remember what he looked like?" asked Lark. "Was he NPS?"

"Yeah." She flailed her arms, signaling the cars creeping up to turn around. "He was tall. Cute, in a craggy sort of way. Like an older, skinnier Ben Affleck. And he had an accent."

The cars and trucks pressed forward. Several drivers pulled into the ditch, throwing dirt off their tires as they peeled around the roadblock. Several others had gotten out of their vehicles and were advancing from the rear. Mob mentality. Lark could read it in their faces. The majority of firefighters worked on a mixture of adrenaline and testosterone. Not a great combination.

Lark exchanged glances with Harry. "What do you think?" she asked. "I'll bet it was Eric."

"That would be my guess." Harry climbed out of his vehicle and headed back to stave off the advancing crew.

"Susie, do you have a radio?" Lark asked.

"In the truck, but —"

Lark didn't wait to hear the end of the sentence. Car horns blared. Voices shouted angry epithets.

Grabbing the radio off the front seat, Lark keyed the mike. "Eric, this is Lark, over."

"I copy," came back.

Relief washed through her at the sound of his voice. She breathed a huge sigh, then said, "We have a situation."

Chapter 7

Eric followed the buses down Highway 66, making sure the road was open and they reached Prospect Point. He turned his truck around a mile short of the pull off. So far the fire had remained clear of the road, but somewhere on the back side of Eagle Cliff Mountain, a fire burned out of control.

Smoke lay thick in the canyon. Ash still tumbled from the sky, reminding him of the day Mount St. Helens erupted. He'd been crossing White Mountain Pass on his way from Seattle to Denver. The smoke and ash created a flat light, then the sky had darkened, turning purplish, and the ash had fallen in blizzard-like conditions. The mountain had made its own storm.

Fire also created weather, generating wind by breathing in oxygen along the ground and spewing it thousands of feet into the air along with smoke and flames. The results were often deadly.

Eric parked on the asphalt. No one except Mountain Search and Rescue would be allowed on the road. They could easily get around him here.

The thought of the missing boys tied his

stomach in knots. It was bad enough to be lost in the woods without the added danger of fire. The nights were cold. Unless one was prepared, hypothermia and dehydration could kill a man overnight.

His thoughts flashed to when he was eleven, living in a house in Lillehammer, Norway. There had been a knock on the door. A policeman stood in the entryway.

There's been an accident, the policeman had told them. Eric's father and three other climbers had been trapped on the mountain by an avalanche. Rescue crews were attempting to reach them, but it was getting dark . . .

Eric shrugged on his pack and clipped his radio to a loop-on strap, making it easier to monitor. If the search team hadn't found the boys by the time he was finished, he'd scout the second ridge looking for them.

He finished checking his tools, repositioned the binoculars, and slammed the car door, when Lark's voice crackled across the radio. Eric turned up the volume. He'd spoken with her earlier regarding the young ranger from the Visitor Center. The situation had been straightened out, he'd put Lark and Harry in charge of the roadblock until an officer showed up to relieve them. Susie had been demoted to backup.

"This is Lark Drummond. Officer Klipp is on scene. Harry Eckles and I are requesting a new assignment, over."

Butch Hanley replied. "Mountain Search and Rescue needs more help up at the Youth Mountain Camp. They have two juveniles missing. You and Harry report there."

"Ten-four."

Eric stepped across the ditch, relieved she wouldn't be on the fire line, disappointed when she signed off. He liked the husky sound of her voice. Face it, he liked her.

Pushing Lark out of his thoughts, Eric scrambled up the embankment and focused on choosing the best route up the mountain. Pasqueflowers sprouted in profusion on the lower hillside. Yellow monkeyflowers grew in clumps beneath groves of aspen. Wind rattled the trees, and Eric watched them sway and bend. Several nesting cavities were visible, but no birds flitted about anywhere. It was as though they sensed impending doom, and had hunkered down.

Turning up the gulch, he braced himself for a climb. Brush and juniper bushes clung to the lower slopes, giving way to heavily forested ground that rose at a six-percent grade.

He'd climbed about a hundred yards, when he thought he heard his name called. He stopped and listened, hearing only the rush of the wind in the trees.

He started climbing again, then stopped, convinced he'd heard his name called again, "Errrrrickkkkkk," the syllables of his name drawn out in a monotone. It was Lark's voice.

"Up here."

He searched for a sign of her below him. "Where?"

A thrashing in the brush precipitated her arrival. Even fire garb accentuated the round curves of her body. Her blond hair was braided loosely down her back, wisps sneaking out to curl gently around her face and soften the harsh edge of the orange hard hat perched on her head. Harry Eckles appeared on her heels.

"What are you two doing here?"

"Ouch," Lark said, either at the tone of his voice or because a branch had scratched her. "I thought you'd be happy to see us."

"You're supposed to be at the Youth Mountain Camp."

"We know," said Harry. "But we saw your truck and thought maybe they'd moved the operation down here."

Eric shook his head. "There's a spot fire burning." He noticed Lark rubbing the ankle she'd broken the summer before. "Are you all right?"

She nodded, spitting on her hand and rubbing vigorously at a spot under her sock near her boot line. "Stinging nettle. So where's this fire?"

"Somewhere up there." He jerked his head toward the summit. "You two should go back."

"Why?" asked Harry. "It looks like you could use some help." Harry patted the head of the Pulaski — a combination hoe and axe tool — that hung from his belt. Eric noticed Lark carried one, too. They must have been outfitted at Prospect Point.

"Because they're expecting you at the Youth Mountain Camp." And because, where he was headed was apt to be dangerous. In all honesty, while he would relish Harry's company, he didn't want to place Lark in any danger.

"We can radio them our change of plans," said Lark, yanking her pant leg down firmly over the top of her boot. "The missing boys headed this way, right? Maybe we can head them off at the pass."

Harry nodded.

She made sense. Short of ordering them to go back and admitting to be the chauvinist he was, Eric had little choice but to notify Butch Hanley that Lark and Harry were with him. If he'd hoped Butch would tell them to report as previously ordered, he was disappointed. The go-ahead was given, and the three of them climbed.

They followed the first wash until it dead-ended in a tangle of juniper and berry bushes and they were forced to backtrack. Not much was said. Everyone seemed to be saving their breath.

The next effort proved more successful.

The second gulch wormed its way up the mountain, the slopes rising steeply on either side. Snags and dead trees littered the hillsides, and they huffed and puffed over fallen logs and around large moss-covered boulders.

"Wait," said Lark.

Eric turned to find her leaning against a large boulder, holding her side. "Tired?"

She made a face, and pointed. Three-quarters of the way up the trunk of a dead pine tree, a male three-toed woodpecker pushed grass into a nesting cavity.

Eric raised his binoculars and trained them on the bird. The black-and-white barring on its sides, flanks and back set it apart from similar species. Its black head, shoulders, wings, and rump appeared inky against the reddish-brown pine. A black tail displayed white outer-tail feathers spotted in black, and it had a white postocular stripe widening on the back of its neck. The three-toed woodpecker turned as though sensing the scrutiny, then cocked its head offering Eric a clear view of its yellow cap and white mustache.

A gust of wind swirled through. The bird departed, and the trio moved on.

They'd only gone a few hundred yards when the landscape changed again. This time due to fire. Flames had ravaged the area. Smoke puddled around their boots, and the smell of charred wood assailed their nostrils. Small campfire-sized fires still burned on the hillside. The soil felt warm.

Eric radioed Hanley. Their location placed them midway up the steep ravine, and Butch told them to start scraping a fire line along the edge of the burn.

"You heard the man," he said. "There are only three of us, and no saws, so we'll diagonal up slope on the south side. Keep the burned area on your right, and keep your eyes open. The fire's up there somewhere."

Pulaskis in hand, Harry and Lark started climbing, scraping a three-foot-wide boundary along the edge of the burned area with the hoe end of the tool. A narrow fire break, but in most cases enough to prevent a flare-up, from jumping into unburned territory.

When Eric didn't follow, Lark stopped digging and turned around. "Aren't you coming?"

"I'll be right behind you." He gestured across the slope toward the other side of the gulch. "I'm going to scout the lower perimeter."

"We'll see you up top," said Harry.

Eric turned back, working downslope along the lower edge of the burn. He wanted to make sure no fire lay below them. Like prevailing winds along a seaboard in the fall, mountain air currents followed patterns. On the coast, the winds surged toward the ocean early in the day to be pulled ashore in the afternoon by heat rising off the land. In the mountains, air flowed downslope in the morning, then roared up the gulches late in the day.

Reaching the bottom of the ravine, Eric started to turn around, when a flash of yellow in the burned-out area caught his attention. Too low to the ground to be a tanager, he thought. Besides, the birds seem to have all fled.

A small spot fire, maybe?

He scrambled closer, skirting a still-glowing stump, following what appeared to be tire tracks in the dirt. Rounding a small boulder, he stopped abruptly. Bile rose in his throat, and he gagged. The charred remains of a body lay sprawled in the soot.

Chapter 8

Eric crabbed his way across the slope, keeping his eye on the body.

Was it one of the missing boys?

He didn't think so, based on the tatters of clothing that had survived the heat. The body appeared to belong to a firefighter.

Eric's heart pounded.

Wayne?

Eric refused to believe it. Wayne might have headed up toward the mountain, but he was too experienced to be caught by the fire.

Nora?

Based on the radio conversation, she'd been out of touch for over an hour.

The closer Eric got to the corpse, the more convinced he was that it wasn't Nora's body. The size and stature suggested it was the body of a man. Then, from a stone's throw, the white hard hat on the ground and the blue-handled Pulaski, identified the victim as Wayne.

Eric dropped one knee to the ground and sucked in great gulps of air in spite of the smell. His boss lay faceup on the ground, bloated and puffed like a turkey after eight hours in a hot oven. The fire had cooked him.

Tears stung Eric's eyes. Wayne had been more than his supervisor, more than a mentor, more than a friend. Wayne had stepped in and taken the place of the father Eric had barely known.

Leaning against a rock, Eric ignored the hard edges gouging his spine. Images filtered through his mind. Wayne at the office, a coffee cup clutched in his hand. Wayne "catch-and-release" fishing at Lily Lake; lounging in the hammock in the backyard; flashing his famous hundred-watt smile at a tourist before stopping traffic to let a herd of Rocky Mountain sheep cross the road.

"Damn it, Wayne."

They'd been friends for seventeen years, since Eric had applied to work in the park. Wayne had seen past the young man who carried a chip on his shoulder and had helped Eric land a job in the park. For that alone Eric owed him.

Eric's first season had been spent building campfires at the Moraine Park Campground. He enforced nightly noise curfews, policed bathrooms, and rousted raccoons out of the trash. Wayne had shown his face only once that summer, in August, when a mother bear and two cubs had hunkered down in the campground. Wayne had chased them off by shooting rubber bullets at the mother bear.

Eric smiled at the memory. The first round had clicked dry, and the mother bear had charged. Jacking the slide, Wayne explained how he always left the chamber empty for added safety.

Now Wayne was dead. Eric exhaled, then licked salt from his lips. There would be plenty of time to grieve. Right now he had a job to do, people to care for. Harry and Lark. Jackie and Tamara.

Eric tugged at his radio. "Butch, Nora, do you copy?"

"Yeah," replied Butch.

"I found Wayne Devlin. He's dead."

"Where? How?" asked Nora. Eric hadn't heard her voice on the radio since Trent had hollered for her, well over an hour ago. He resisted asking her where she had been.

"Welcome back," he said.

When she didn't respond, he gave his approximate location. "From the best I can tell, Wayne got caught in the spot fire."

"I'll get someone up there as soon as I can," replied Nora.

"What about Jackie?" Eric asked, worried Linda Verbiscar or some other member of the press might grab hold of the story and start snooping around.

"I'll send someone over to tell her."

"Sounds like a plan."

"Are you okay?" The question sounded sincere.

"I'm numb." Blood pounding in his ears filled his head with a dull roar. "I left Lark and Harry digging fire line. I need to catch up to them."

"Maybe you need to stand down."

Was she ordering him off the job? The roaring grew louder, and he realized that what he was hearing was not the pulsing of blood, but the wind driving fire. "Shit."

"What?"

He stared up at the ridge line. A column of black smoke spiraled toward a sky tinged yellow by advancing flame. He watched as fire crowned in the trees to the left of him. He dropped the radio. It caught on its hook and slammed against his chest, knocking the wind out of him. Scrambling up the north slope, binoculars banging against his ribs, he yelled for Lark and Harry. Brush tore at his clothing, scratching his bared wrist. Jumping over a fallen log, he scraped his shin. Hand over Pulaski, he clawed his way up the mountain.

"Eric?" Nora's voice blared from the radio.

He ignored her, shouting for Lark.

"Up here," she answered.

He caught a flash of yellow through the trees. The arc of her arm. She and Harry had hacked their way twenty-five yards up the hillside.

Behind Eric, heat wafted up from the bottom of the gulch. Oppressive, unbearable heat. Arid and scorching, like the kind that rose in waves from the rocks of a sauna.

Eric's mouth went dry.

Harry stood above Lark on the slope, his expression indicating he had seen the blowup. He stared, mesmerized, at the spectacle, and Eric fought a desire to look behind him. From the corner of his eye he could see flames curling and whipping as they hooked up the slope. There wasn't time enough to turn around. Maybe not even time enough to run.

"Get into the black, now," Eric ordered. "Now!"

The words snapped Harry free of the spell, and he moved, darting for the safety zone.

Eric reached Lark and pushed her ahead of him onto charred ground. If Wag Dodge, the foreman on the Mann Gulch Fire, could save himself by lying down on the freshly burned ground, maybe they could too. Pushing Lark farther and farther into the black, Eric prayed for a miracle.

Scrambling over logs still glowing with embers, he listened to the roar of the fire grow. Like a high-speed passenger train, it roared toward them, drawn like a magnet to the spot fire burning somewhere uphill, the gulch acting as a chimney. The ravine boiled in fire, jets of flame shooting into the crowns of the trees. A wall of flame roiled toward them, burning everything in its path.

Harry stumbled and fell.

"Deploy," shouted Eric. "Deploy!"

He dug in his pack for the foil shelter, and ripped it free of its plastic cover. On his order, Lark and Harry had done the same. At this moment, bunched together on the charred hillside, each of them was on their own.

Eric anchored the shelter with his toes, yanking it over his back and pinning it to the ground in front of him with gloved hands. Embers pelted the flimsy tent. Wind ripped at the edges, spitting bits of charcoal into his face. Rifle shots rang through the air, the sound of trees exploding. The ground felt hot, his lungs burned, and he pushed his face closer to the charred dirt, rooting for cooler air.

He thought of Lark, and Harry, and Wayne. He thought of his mother in Lillehammer, and how angry she would be if he died. He thought of Jackie and Tamara, and, inexplicably, of a Norwegian potty-training song that his grandmother used to sing.

The wind took on the whine of a jet engine. Trees popped like firecrackers. The inside of the fire shelter glowed. Eric felt a sudden crushing weight as the fire rolled over them. He arched, cringing away from the heat, away from the death he feared. Then the roar diminished, the pressure ebbed, and the train passed on.

He lay quietly.

Nora's voice crackled from the radio, then

Lark called out. "Eric?"

"Don't get out."

"Trust me," she said.

He smiled at the sarcasm in her voice. Humor served as first aid cream for the soul.

"Harry," he shouted. "Are you there?"

"Present and accounted for."

"Everyone stay covered," Eric ordered. "The worst is over, but there's still fire out there." He could feel its heat through the foil and see the glow under the edges of his tent. "It'll be hot. We're safer inside."

"Now I know why they call them 'brown and serve bags,'" Harry said.

Lark giggled, hysteria bubbling close to the surface. "I thought they were called 'shake 'n' bakes.'"

"Same difference."

Eric thought of Wayne. He didn't remember seeing any sign that Wayne had tried to deploy his shelter. No bag on the ground. Had he been caught that unaware?

The others didn't know about Wayne, and Eric decided he should wait to tell them. Right now, wasn't the time to speculate on what had happened. He needed to maintain morale.

Eric maneuvered the radio out from under him and notified Nora they were okay, turning down the volume in case she said something about Wayne.

"You guys hang tight."

"*Ja,* we'll do that."

The three of them hollered back and forth for what seemed like close to an hour before Eric's shelter cooled enough so that he felt like sticking his head out from under the foil. After a tentative test, he sounded the all clear.

Harry peeled back his covering, shaking away the soot like a wet dog sheds water. His face, sandy hair, and clothes were still covered in ash.

"I should look so good," said Eric.

"You might be surprised."

Lark refused to come out.

"It's okay," said Harry.

"I feel safer in here."

Eventually, she loosened her grip on the shelter, and Eric unwrapped her. Her blue eyes peered up at him from a blackened face streaked by tears.

"Oh, God," she said, and he enveloped her in his arms. Sobs racked her body, and she wheezed and coughed. Finally, after a few minutes, she pulled away, wiping her face on her sleeve. "Sorry."

"Hey, at least you waited until after the crisis to fall apart," said Harry.

Eric brushed back a loose strand of her hair, thought of kissing her, then pushed himself up from the ground. "Does everyone still have their tools?"

Harry and Lark both raised their Pulaskis.

"Good, now here's what's happened." Eric filled them in about Wayne. Lark cried again. Harry looked pained. "We're going to hike back down the draw to his body. Keep your hard hats on. The biggest danger now is falling branches."

The landscape looked surreal. Smoke eddied about the forest floor, like ground fog, and small fires burned all around them. Stumps flamed like candles. Logs smoldered, threatening to combust at the slightest provocation. Nora radioed to let them know a park law enforcement officer and ambulance crew were on their way.

"What about the boys?" Eric had asked. She told him they were still missing.

As they hiked down the mountain, a cushion of ash stirred with every footstep, reminding Eric of the footage of Neil Armstrong's walk on the moon. Imprints pressed into feather-fine dust, left a preliminary record that man had conquered his environment. Remnants of trees twisted by fire hovered like turkey vultures over ground littered with the bones of smoldering logs. Heat hazed the air. Oddly, in some places clumps of trees stood untouched, spared from the onslaught.

Tornadoes did that. Touched down, skipping over one home, wreaking havoc on another. Mother Nature unleashing her fury judiciously, or by chance.

Eric led them to where he'd found Wayne's body. Amazingly, the fire had jumped between hillsides, skipping over the bottom of the ravine in its race to the top of the next hill, sparing an assault on the already dead. A small consolation.

Harry started forward, but Eric warned him back. There would be an investigation, and they needed to leave the scene intact. Hanging behind the others, Lark volunteered to go down and lead the ambulance crew up the hill.

Pacey Trent had arrived with the ambulance crew, a Park Service law enforcement officer, several sheriff's deputies, and a twenty-man crew. The area was cordoned off, yellow crime scene tape wrapped around anything that hadn't burned.

"We'll take it from here," said Trent. "You three look like you could use some rest."

Eric looked at the others. "If it's all the same to you, sir, I'd like to help look for the missing boys."

Lark and Harry exchanged glances. "Us, too."

They joined the search at three, and by nine o'clock the teenagers still hadn't been found. With the onset of night, the humidity rose, the fire laid down, and Butch Hanley had declared it under control. Fifty percent contained, with a promise of full containment by the following afternoon. Doable, based on forecasts calling for rain or light snow.

An hour past dark, Vic had called off the search. Lark and Harry headed into town with the other rescue team members. Eric had parked himself in a leather rocking chair on the veranda of the Youth Mountain Camp lodge. He needed some time to think about things, about the day's events, about Wayne Devlin's untimely death. Maybe talking to Vic would help.

Anger welled up inside him when he remembered that no one had listened to him earlier when he'd expressed concern over Wayne's absence. Maybe if someone had and they'd sent out a search party Wayne wouldn't be dead. Maybe if Eric himself hadn't been so easy to convince. Maybe.

To the north, Eagle Cliff Mountain still glowed. The fire had settled down into hundreds of small fires dotting the mountaintop. The fires ranged in size, anywhere from pickup truck-sized to as small as a campfire you'd roast marshmallows over. Eric would lay odds that somewhere up there a firefighter was roasting hot dogs.

"Whew," said Vic, joining him on the porch. "I am sure glad this day is over." He sat down rubbing his eyes, then stroked his hand over his mustache.

"Me, too." Eric rocked, gently, mostly because the chair sat low to the ground and his knees folded close to his chest with the motion. He jerked his head toward the mountain. "Do you think those boys are up there?"

"Nope."

"Me either."

"If you want my opinion, those boys lit out for home. It won't surprise me if they pick them up in Castle Rock tomorrow."

Eric remembered Vic saying one of the boys was from that area. "What's the story behind these kids, anyway?"

"You mean all of the kids, or the two that are missing?"

"Either. Both."

Vic settled back in his chair. "The Youth Mountain Camp is tied to a mentoring program run by the city and county of Denver. Our primary goal is to provide a mountain experience to kids from the inner city. Most of our campers have been in some sort of trouble, usually minor offenses. These kids are more in need of guidance than anything else."

"Do the mentors spend time up here?"

"We try." From the disappointment in his voice, Eric guessed not many of the police officers found time.

"Didn't you spend some time up here as a kid?" Eric knew the question was personal, but asked anyway.

"Yes."

A one-syllable answer. Eric knew if he re-phrased, he could force more of an answer, then decided he didn't know the sheriff well enough to press. "What about the —"

Vic interrupted. "My 'Big Brother' was a Denver policeman. He signed me up for a week, and I fell in love with the place. After that summer, I vowed I'd live in Elk Park." He held his arms wide. "Here I am."

Rumors run rampant in small towns. Elk Park was no exception. The story was, when Vic was sixteen, he had witnessed his father's murder in a domestic dispute, and the trauma had triggered some wild behavior in Vic.

"Is what they say true?" asked Eric, curiosity tromping on good manners.

"About my dad?"

Eric nodded. Faint light shining through the windows, sliced across Vic's face. Old pain shadowed his eyes.

"Yes." Another one-syllable answer. Vic pushed out of his chair. "Want a beer?"

"Sure."

While the sheriff scrounged through the refrigerator, Eric repositioned himself in the chair. Stretching his legs in front of him, he rested his head on the back of the chair and dragged a hand through his hair. It felt matted, sticky from the heat. He should be home taking a shower. Or at Devlin's house, offering comfort to Jackie and Tamara. He owed it to Wayne.

"Don't beat yourself up, son. Everybody needs time to process grief in their own way." The sheriff handed him a can of Coors.

The cold felt good against his palms, and for the first time Eric realized his hands had been blistered in the fire.

"Wayne was a good man," said Vic.

"That he was." Eric raised his can in toast, and the two of them slugged down some beer.

"Is what they say about him true?"

"*Ja.*"

Vic waited, so Eric continued. "Something was going on with him. I'm not sure what. He missed work sometimes, like he forgot he had to be there. Only, he could never tell you where he'd been."

"Maybe he had a girlfriend?"

Eric weighed the possibility. "I don't think so. He seemed pretty devoted to Jackie."

"What about doctor's appointments?"

Eric cocked his head and stared at Vic. Did the sheriff know something Eric didn't? "Not that I knew about."

Vic cradled his beer in his lap. "You know, men hit a certain age, and there are problems we don't want to discuss."

Eric let the comment pass, but made a mental note to check it out with Jackie. Changing the subject, he said, "Tell me about the two boys."

Vic narrowed his eyes, then shrugged. "There isn't much I can say. Their criminal records are confidential. The camp doesn't even try to order them up anymore." He rubbed his chin. "But if you're asking my opinion . . . of the two of them, Justin Suett's the bigger problem."

Eric closed his eyes, picturing the dorm room photograph. "The scrawny kid, with the blond hair?"

"Nope. You've scrambled them. Suett's the real all-American type. A real charmer. But there's something not right about him. You can see it in his eyes." Vic drained his beer, then crushed the can. "Well," he said, standing up, "you'll have to excuse me. I've got to get into town, check on some campers."

"I should go too." Eric jimmied himself out of the chair. His muscles screamed from the exertion, and he straightened himself up like an old man. "Are you searching some more tomorrow?"

"Not unless Crandall insists. I don't see any point in it. We've put out an APB. Eventually those boys'll surface."

"Well, let me know if you need help."

Vic put a hand on Eric's shoulder. "I appreciate that, Eric. You're a good man."

Driving toward Elk Park, the words reverberated in Eric's head. He slowed near the spot where he'd parked his truck earlier and parked on the side of the road. Thoughts of Wayne triggered the sting of hot tears, and Eric's memory of the day they'd found his father's body. Eric had braced himself against the cold and listened as the officer confirmed that his father was dead. His mother had collapsed, and the officer had helped carry her into the bedroom, leaving her in Eric's charge. It was a role he'd relished, and one he hadn't relinquished with dignity on the day of her marriage to Lars.

Twenty-three years had slipped by since then. He'd patched up his relationship with his mother, called a truce with Lars, and found a surrogate father in Wayne.

Now, Wayne was dead, and he felt eleven years old again. Certainly not like a man. More like an injured child. In thirty-four years, he'd never truly grown up.

Chapter 9

Cecilia Meyer and Dorothy MacBean were sitting on the front porch of the carriage house when Lark pulled up in the pickup.

"What are you ladies doing here?" asked Lark, clumping up the steps.

"We wanted to hear the story firsthand."

Leave it to Dorothy to get right to the point.

Both women leaned in anxiously. They were sisters and mirror images of each other, despite the two years that separated them. In their sixties, they colored their hair the same mouse-brown shade, wearing it stylishly permed and cropped just below the ears. They had the same pale skin and gray eyes. The only discernible difference between them was that Cecilia loved the color blue, and Dorothy preferred pink.

Lark stepped into the beam of the porch light. "I don't think I'm up for this."

Cecilia gasped. "Are you okay?"

"I'm fine."

"Well, you need a bath."

"Tell me about it."

"We heard that Wayne Devlin's dead," said Dorothy. "Have you heard anything about the Wildland Center?"

Located off of Highway 66, Dorothy Mac-Bean's pet project, the multimillion-dollar Wildland Center, had only recently opened. A controversial education facility, it comingled informational displays on the wild-life and habitats of Colorado with zoo-like exhibits of the more exotic animals of the area. Lark knew Dorothy had been filling in as an assistant to the CEO, Forest Nettleman.

"No one said," Lark answered.

"Dottie," interjected Cecilia. "Let's give her a chance to clean up." She opened the screen door and shooed Lark into the kitchen. "Just drop the pack, and we'll take care of it. And we'll make you some tea and something to eat while you go take a shower."

"Bath," Lark corrected. Cecilia had been right the first time.

Lark stripped in the laundry room. When she saw the state of her clothes, she wondered what the front seat of her pickup looked like. She'd probably have to vacuum it before driving anywhere tomorrow.

Luckily, she didn't have to go back out on the fire. Butch Hanley had announced that the seasonal fire crews would handle the mop-up. That meant Eric would be out there working, but not the majority of volunteers.

She wondered how he was doing. He had walked her out to the truck when she left, squeezing her shoulder and telling her to drive carefully. He had looked so forlorn that she'd hesitated to go, but there was something about his manner that told her it was better to go and leave him to his private bereavement. That this was something he had to work through on his own.

For all the sadness of the day, Lark laughed when she saw herself in the mirror. Her hair, face, neck, and hands were black with soot, except for a bowl-shaped circle of blond hair left where her hard hat had covered her head and circles around her eyes where her goggles had been. She looked like a raccoon with large blue eyes.

Cecilia was right. Shower first.

Allowing the water to wash away the grime, she luxuriated in the comfort of the heat and steam, her skin soaking in the moisture like a needy sponge. She shampooed her hair twice, scoured the porcelain, then drew a tub full of water.

The wait proved to be too much for the sisters. Lark had no sooner settled under the bubbles, when Dorothy knocked on the bathroom door. "Are you almost finished in there?"

"Give me a few more minutes?" Lark asked.

"The tea is ready."

"I'll be right there." Lark compromised. She soaked for a minute more, then reluctantly pulled the drain plug and struggled up out of the bath. Her muscles ached with a soreness that went straight to the bone. Toweling dry and putting on pajamas required monumental effort, which was rewarded by hot tea and a chicken pot pie.

"So . . . ," prompted Dorothy, once she sat down at the kitchen table. "Tell us what happened up there."

The women flanked her, scooting their chairs up to the table and leaning forward.

"It was scary," said Lark. "And awful."

She processed the emotions of the day as she recounted the events. Laughter spilled out when she described the encounter with Ranger Susie; anxiety tightened her muscles, as she recalled the firestorm, and she found herself clinging to the edges of her seat. Talking about Wayne Devlin proved the hardest.

Lark hadn't ventured near the body. Twice in the past year she'd had occasion to see dead people. Once in the thicket when her friend Rachel Stanhope had stumbled over the body of Donald Bursau, a reporter from *Birds of a Feather* magazine. And once when her partner Esther Mills had been stabbed behind the Warbler Café. The first time she'd thrown up in the bushes. The second, she'd kept her distance, and almost thrown up. This time she'd positioned a large rock between herself and the deceased, and breathed.

Harry'd been all business, but Eric had been visibly shaken. He had been close friends with Wayne, practically a member of the Devlin family. Lark had known Wayne in passing, and Jackie only slightly better, because of chance encounters in the grocery store and the café.

"I wonder how Jackie and Tamara are doing," said Dorothy, settling back in her chair.

"And to think," added Cecilia. "She was just in the Warbler today, buying him coffee."

"She's apt to want a refund." The words popped out, and Lark buried her face in her napkin. "I can't believe I said that."

"You're just tired," said Cecilia charitably. "Dottie and I should go."

"No, wait," said Lark. "I want to hear your stories."

Cecilia didn't have much to say. She'd stayed at the Warbler, picking up tidbits from the tourists. An occasional news broadcast flashed an update of the fire's progress, but the information tended to be repetitious.

"Then Dottie came in looking like a scared rabbit, and —"

"I was not scared." Dorothy put on her best schoolmarm expression and turned to Lark. "I may have looked flushed, and I was worried about the Wildland Center, but . . ." She glared at Cecilia. "I was *not* scared."

104

Lark stuffed a forkful of pot pie in her mouth to keep from laughing.

"Anyway, there's nothing to tell. I went into work early and found Forest already there. He must have come in at the crack of dawn, because the paper, which gets delivered around seven o'clock, was still on the front stoop."

Lark suspected that Dorothy had a crush on Forest Nettleman. Something in the way she uttered his name. A rabid environmentalist, Forest had been a U.S. congressman, representing the 4th District, up until last year when a reporter had exposed his involvement in the illegal trading of peregrine falcons to a sheik in the Middle East. The scandal had put him on the sidelines. Then, despite his ignoble behavior, he'd been hired as CEO of the Wildland Center by vote of an overwhelming majority of the board of directors, and he'd found himself with a new career. Dorothy's support of him had been unwavering.

"The police department called and ordered us to evacuate, around quarter to eleven. Forest had already gone home, and I headed straight to the Warbler."

Their conversation spent, the threesome lapsed into a companionable silence. The sisters helped do the dishes, then bid Lark goodnight. Lark headed straight to bed.

Awake early the next morning, she tried

calling Eric before heading to work, and got his answering machine.

"Just checking in," she said, after the beep. "I'll be in my office. Call me later."

When she showed up at the Drummond, Stephen acted overjoyed to see her. She spent the morning plowing through the paperwork on her desk; then, at noon, stopped for lunch, flipping on the TV to catch the latest on the fire.

"This is Linda Verbiscar reporting for KEPC-TV." A blond woman in a bright pink suit and matching shoes faced the camera. Behind her was a live shot of Eagle Cliff Mountain on fire.

"At a press conference this morning, Pacey Trent, the Intermountain Regional fire management officer for the National Park Service, and incident commander on what's now being called the Eagle Cliff Fire, announced the death of Wayne Devlin. An eighteen-year employee of the National Park Service, Devlin died yesterday under suspicious circumstances."

Lark reached for the television controls and turned the volume up. What was suspicious about a fireman dying in a fire?

"According to investigators, Devlin, who was supposed to have served as the 'burn boss' in yesterday's prescribed burn, never reported for work. His body was discovered in a gulch on the backside of Eagle Cliff Moun-

106

tain at approximately noon yesterday."

The camera flashed to a studio anchorman. "Is there any speculation on what may have been the cause of his death?"

"Dan, an autopsy is under way," said Verbiscar, tucking a strand of hair behind one ear. "But my source within the Park Service revealed that there may be reason to believe Wayne Devlin died as the result of a fire *he* himself may have started."

Lark and the anchorman both sat up straighter.

"Exactly what does that mean?"

Verbiscar turned, facing the camera more squarely. "A little background for the viewers, Dan. According to NPS policy, if an employee working for the Park Service is found negligent in his duties, and that negligence results in the death of someone, or in the destruction of property; then the negligent employee becomes the liable party in the event some sort of restitution of damages is required."

"So are you saying, then, that Wayne Devlin, if found responsible, could be held liable in his own death?"

Verbiscar hesitated. "Seriously, Dan, I doubt if his family would try and collect against him. However, his insurance company might. According to my source, it is possible Wayne Devlin's estate could be attached for the damages caused by the Eagle Cliff Fire."

"What is the official Park Service line?"

Verbiscar remained silent for an extra beat. "Officials here have reserved comment until the investigation into just what did cause the fire that may have killed Devlin is complete. Back to you, Dan."

The anchorman filled the screen. "There you have the latest from the scene of the Eagle Cliff Fire, where over nine thousand acres have burned. Before this fire was contained, several hundred people were forced to evacuate, many of them teenagers, two developments have been destroyed — the Shangri-la housing development, a model development showcasing upscale homes, and the Wildland Center, a multimillion-dollar complex just recently opened — and, as you've now heard, one man is dead.

"In other related news, there is still no sign of the two teenage boys missing from the area, and the mop-up effort continues. Firefighters are . . ."

Lark hit the mute button. This did not bode well.

Chapter 10

Eric spent two days supervising mop-up on the Eagle Cliff Fire. There had been flare-ups — pockets of fire the warm days breathed to life — but then a late spring snow had crushed the embers out of the smoldering logs, and the Eagle Cliff Fire was officially declared "controlled."

Slogging down from the mountain's summit, he listened for the crack of branches overhead. Snags breaking under the weight of high-moisture snow had been known to kill a man, and he didn't relish becoming a victim. Walking was treacherous, the charred earth denuded of undergrowth churned to mud under his feet, and he chose his path carefully, not wanting to add to the erosion.

He jumped down the embankment to the pull out where he'd parked and was surprised to find Pacey Trent waiting beside his truck. Eric slowed his pace. By the expression on Trent's face, whatever business he had with Eric wasn't good.

As soon as he came within range, Trent stepped forward. "I thought you might like to see a copy of the investigation team's report regarding Wayne Devlin's death," he said, waving a packet of papers. "We're still waiting on the autopsy, but the coroner gave me the results over the phone."

Eric pitched his hard hat and pack into the back of his truck, and waited. Presumably, there was a punch line.

"It seems Wayne died from a blow to the head," said Trent. He cleared his throat and looked toward the mountain. "In the most likely scenario, he slipped, or stumbled, then fell down and smashed his head on a rock."

Eric sensed there was more to it, something Trent *wasn't* saying.

"So he wasn't caught when the spot fire swept through?" Remembering the hour he'd spent in the fire shelter — the searing heat, the hot air, the falling embers — Eric took some comfort in at least knowing Wayne hadn't burned alive.

"Not exactly. There is some evidence of smoke inhalation, but it's not what killed him." Trent tapped the report, then thrust it into Eric's hands. "Everything's in here. I suggest you take a gander."

Eric must have looked confused, for Trent reiterated. "Take a *look.*"

Again, the unspoken inference that there was something more to it. Was he thinking Wayne's death wasn't an accident?

An engine revved, and Eric turned in time to see Nora Frank bounce her truck onto the charred dirt. She goosed the gas, crushing a

110

surviving sagebrush plant dusted in snow. What the fire hadn't destroyed, man would. Maybe he was asking too much to hope a plant survey might find some bitterbrush intact.

Eric focused on the report. It was mostly a listing of physical evidence. Wayne's clothes were cataloged — remnants of boots, socks, underwear, a T-shirt, Nomex shirt and pants, all covered in bits of plant and wood materials consistent with where the body was found, along with several charred fibers that could easily have come from the seat of his pickup truck.

Oddly enough, the pickup had never been located. Either Wayne had parked it in a well-hidden spot, or someone else had come along and borrowed it. There was no mention of any keys found in the report. But then, it was possible Wayne had left them in the ignition, figuring he wouldn't be gone long enough for someone to make off with his truck.

A pack found near a tree stump several yards from the body had contained remains of all the expected items: a hard hat, goggles, canteen, fire shelter, snacks, two fusees, a radio, and a knife.

One item was missing from the list. The weather kit. Jackie had said Wayne left early to test the humidity on Eagle Cliff Mountain. He would have needed a psychrometer to do that.

Eric skimmed the remaining pages. Wayne had been wearing his gloves, and residue from a fusee was found on the leather. There was no mention of a wet-and-dry bulb kit anywhere.

He leaned back against the side of his truck. Something about the report bothered him. Something more than the missing pickup truck, or the missing psychrometer.

"So, what do you think?" asked Nora, strolling toward them, her tone casual. Too casual.

His gut gnawed at him. Rather than answering, he countered back with a question. "What am I supposed to think? It's thorough."

"Come on, Linenger. Dig deeper," Nora prodded. She seemed to be enjoying herself immensely. "Give us your take on it. Notice anything out of whack?"

Eric wet his lips and glanced between the two supervisors. What the heck? "I noticed there's no mention of his pickup being found."

Eric remembered seeing tire tracks near the body. Maybe that's what chewed at his stomach. He flipped through the report and came up empty.

"There was a vehicle up there," he said. "I saw the tracks myself. There's no mention of them in here."

"I don't remember seeing any when I arrived," said Trent.

"They were there," Eric insisted. "Maybe the firestorm obliterated them."

Nora shifted her weight from one foot to the other. "You're not suggesting Wayne drove his pickup in there, are you?"

"Are you inferring some sort of foul play?" asked Trent.

Eric's gaze drifted to the charred and spindly trees on the northern slope. A tight fit for a truck, but not impossible if you came at it from different angles. "It would explain why his vehicle hasn't been found."

Nora scoffed at the idea. "Those tracks probably came from someone screwing around on an ATV."

Eric had to admit there was that possibility. Even with an excess of rules and regulations, some riders ignored the laws. In the summer, rangers struggled with keeping all terrain vehicles out of the woods, and, in the winter, snowmobiles. Areas that bumped up against the national forest, or private lands, were more susceptible.

"Possibly, but that doesn't address the whereabouts of the missing vehicle," Eric countered.

Nora shrugged. "Yeah, but it's my guess he drove it into the trees a ways, then hoofed it from there. I'll put a few seasonals on it now that the fire's out, and we'll find it."

An expression of annoyance, or was it distrust, flashed across Trent's face. "All right," he said. "I'm going to get right to the point. The fire on Eagle Cliff Mountain appears to have started in a pile of slash a few feet from where we found Devlin's body. Investigators found fusee residue around the branches." He met Eric's gaze. "Devlin had fusee residue on his gloves."

It took Eric a second or two to absorb the information. What he heard didn't make sense. "Are you suggesting Wayne built a campfire?"

"More like a bonfire," said Nora.

Trent shot her another look.

Eric's mind rebelled. Wayne had been worried about the dry conditions and had gone up on the mountain to test the humidity. There was no way he would have lit a fire. No reason to have done so.

"I don't believe it."

"The evidence is there, Linenger," said Nora. "Wayne had the fusee in his hand. Hey, who knows? Maybe he cracked and went off the deep end. Even you have to admit he'd been acting rather strange lately."

A chill flashed along Eric's spine.

"Besides, it doesn't matter *why* he did it," she continued. "Based on the report," she jerked her head toward the papers still clutched in Eric's hand, "we can now officially state that Wayne was the one responsible for the Eagle Cliff Fire."

"Blame shifting?" Eric regretted the words the minute they popped out.

Nora stiffened.

"Sorry. That wasn't fair."

Or was it? While Nora had not been the only one anxious to light the burn, she now seemed the most intent on pointing the finger at Wayne. In a broadcast two days ago, Linda Verbiscar had alluded to Wayne's culpability, quoting a "source within the Park Service." Had she been referring to Nora Frank? Or maybe the Intermountain Regional FMO?

Eric turned to Trent. "You aren't seriously considering dumping this burden on Wayne's family, are you?"

Trent stared down, worrying a charred stick with the toe of his boot — a boot still shiny under a thin coat of dust. "You have to understand, Eric, the National Park Service is in a precarious position."

Trent looked up, his eyes haunted. Was it forgiveness he wanted?

"You know how long there's been a federal no-burn policy," he said. "We've only just opened the door for fire management burns."

"So you're going to absolve the Park Service by accusing Wayne Devlin of intentionally lighting the fire?" Anger torqued through Eric. He felt his blood pressure jump. "After eighteen years, you're just going to trash his reputation and destroy his service record?"

He frowned. "And what happens if Paxton or the Wildland Center files a lawsuit?"

"His family could lose his pension," Nora answered.

"She's right," agreed Trent. "Any judgment could take the pension and put his personal effects at risk."

"*Ja.* You do know he has a daughter graduating from high school this year? Have you thought about how this will affect her?"

"Guess her *daddy* should have thought about that," Nora spat out the words, and Eric figured she was still angry over his "blame-shifting" comment.

Trent cut her off by raising his hand. "Again, Eric, try and see this from my point of view. The Eagle Cliff Fire burned an additional two thousand acres of park land. It destroyed over five hundred acres of national forest and an untold amount of private use land. Damage estimates are in the tens of millions of dollars, and that doesn't include the cost of the firefighting efforts, or law enforcement hours attributable to the fire, *or* housing and feeding the two hundred people who were forced to evacuate." Trent shook his head. "The investigation proves that Wayne Devlin lit the fire. Unfortunately, it's out of my hands."

Eric turned away, a sickening thought seeping through his anger. What if Nora was right about Wayne snapping? There was no disputing he'd been acting strangely. What if he'd known something was wrong with him, something terrible, and decided to make a bid for the "101 Club"?

When a firefighter died in the line of duty, their family became eligible for benefits through the Public Safety Officers' Benefit Act. Passed in 1949, in the wake of the Mann Gulch Fire, the act provided that one hundred thousand dollars in tax-free money be paid to surviving children and spouses. With inflation, the current payout amount was upwards of one hundred fifty thousand dollars. If Wayne had wanted to add a bonus to his pension benefits, dying in a fire would do it. It would also account for the fact that he hadn't used or answered his radio.

"Have you told Jackie and Tamara yet?" Eric asked.

"I . . . we thought . . ." Trent's words stumbled to a halt. "There'll be a press conference this afternoon. I thought, considering how close you were to Devlin, that maybe you'd want to be the one to give a heads-up to the family."

Wimping out? Eric narrowed his eyes at Trent. "That's Nora's responsibility."

"We . . . I thought it might come easier from you," said Trent. "Guess it's your call."

Eric glanced at Nora, standing with her arms crossed, her hands clenched into tight fists. Then he glanced down at Trent's shiny boots.

"*Ja*, I'll talk to Jackie," said Eric. Better than either of them. Besides, he owed it to Wayne.

Chapter 11

Wet, dirty, and depressed, Eric stopped off at home on his way to see Jackie. Even the sight of the cabin lifted his spirits.

Centered on ten acres of land with views of the park, the cabin had taken two years to design and three years to build. He'd hired contractors to put in a gravel driveway and dig the well. Then with Wayne Devlin's help, he'd laid the subfloor, pieced together the external log and mortar structure, insulated, and installed white pine walls and floors in the interior. Solar cells provided energy to the generator, and inside they'd equipped the home with energy-efficient appliances — a wood-burning fireplace, a propane stove, and a composting toilet imported from Norway. As a finishing touch, Wayne had suggested galvanized steel for baseboards, cupboards, panel trim, and countertops — giving the cabin the feel of an early settler's home.

The two of them had spent a lot of time here, working together. Now the cabin stood as a testament to their friendship.

Eric left his pack in the truck and peeled off his sooty work clothes in the mud room. Stuffing them into the washing machine, he climbed into the shower and let the hot spray rinse away the grime, cleansing his body, if not his soul. When the hot water was exhausted, he shaved, pulled on a pair of clean jeans, a "Save the Rainforest" T-shirt he'd bought at the Migration Alliance convention last summer, and a pair of tennis shoes. Then, he grabbed a bottle of water from the refrigerator and headed back out.

The Devlins lived a mile farther up the road, and Eric decided to hoof it. Nothing cleared the mind like walking, and he was seeking alternatives to the inevitable.

But no matter how he worried the details, the end result was the same. As far as the investigation team and the National Park Service were concerned, Wayne had started the fire that burned Shangri-la and the Wildland Center to the ground. Why didn't seem to matter. How he would explain it to Jackie was his problem.

The Devlin house sprawled at the edge of a small meadow, a flat, ranch-style house with a wide front porch reminiscent of a southern veranda. A split-rail fence ringed the property to keep in two quarter horses that grazed behind the three-car attached garage, which doubled as a barn from the backside.

Jackie answered the front door before he knocked. Slipping outside onto the front porch, she shut the door, blocking his entrance. Draped in black silk, she looked pale in spite of a faint dusting of red rouge on her cheeks, and the lack of sleep had carved dark circles under her eyes. She leaned against the door, resting her hand on the doorknob.

"This isn't the best time, Eric. Tamara's finally resting."

"We have to talk, Jackie."

Her eyes narrowed. "What's so important it can't wait?"

"Maybe we should go inside and sit down." The line smacked of cliché, but he couldn't think of anything else to say.

"Why?" Her frown deepened. "What's this all about?"

"I really think —"

"Just tell me, Eric," she ordered, her fingers tightening on the doorknob.

Realizing Jackie had no intentions of letting him in, Eric paced the length of the top step, searching for words to soften the blow. He settled on the truth. "The Park Service is holding a press conference in an hour. They're going to say Wayne is responsible for the Eagle Cliff Fire. They're going to say he set it on purpose, without authority or reason."

The color drained from Jackie's face, her makeup taking on a masklike quality. "That's absurd."

"Not according to the investigation team's report."

Eric filled her in on the gist of his conversation with Pacey Trent and Nora. Then, feeling guilty for harboring his own sliver of doubt, he searched for something more to say. "I tried to talk Trent into holding off on the announcement for a day or two, but he wouldn't. He says it's settled. NPS is going official with the team's findings on the evening news."

Jackie released the doorknob, and the door swung open. Afraid she might collapse, Eric looped his arm around her back and steered her toward a couch in the living room.

Decorative, and mostly unused, the room had a plastic-wrapped feeling that made him uneasy. Two white leather couches adorned with colored pillows centered the room. End tables of metal and glass, inlaid wood floors, and an empty fireplace stuffed with a mass of bird's-nest ferns lent the room a "Parade of Homes" quality. The crowning touch was a pair of lead-crystal candlesticks gracing the mantel.

Given a choice, he preferred the coziness of the Devlins' kitchen. He couldn't count the number of nights he'd scooted in around the worn mahogany table — Wayne and him drinking coffee and swapping stories, while Tamara watched TV in the adjoining family room and smells of Jackie's baking permeated the air.

"It's bad enough he's gone," she said, her

voice slicing through his memories. "Now they're going to force us into bankruptcy."

"You don't know that." Sitting opposite Jackie, Eric reached for her hands. They felt ice cold. Gently, he rubbed them, searching for something to say, finding only the question he dreaded asking.

"Jackie, was there something wrong with Wayne? Was he sick?"

She snatched her hands away, folding them on her black skirt and tapping the pads of her thumbs together. "Why do you ask?"

Eric cringed. The truth was, the idea Wayne might have started the fire — intending to make it look like he'd died in the line of duty — had entrenched itself in the back of Eric's mind. And something Wayne had said to him less than two weeks ago reinforced the thought.

The two of them had been checking a fish ladder on the Big Thompson River. They'd needed a wrench, so Wayne had gone back to the office to fetch one. He'd never returned. Eric had hiked out and found him at home, ensconced in a lawn chair with a Tom Clancy novel. Wayne had sworn he'd never been on the job.

When Eric had asked him if he was okay, Wayne had shaken his head. "No, I'm not sure I am. But, don't you worry about me, Eric. This old job is going to take care of Wayne Devlin."

It was a comment anyone nearing retirement might have made, but Wayne still had two years to go. Eric wondered now if maybe he'd meant something else.

"Well?" asked Jackie. She was watching him closely. "You think they're on to something, don't you?"

The horror in her voice made him want to backpedal and retract the question. Instead, he forged on.

"We've talked about Wayne's behavior."

She turned her face away.

"Just hear me out, Jackie."

An instant replay of their conversations made Eric realize that most of them had taken place after unsettling incidents. And most had been one-sided — him digging for information, and Jackie or Wayne stonewalling. But after the fish ladder incident Jackie had pulled him aside, admitting she was worried. According to her, Wayne hadn't been feeling well. Yet, all Eric had gleaned was that Wayne suffered from high cholesterol and skyrocketing triglycerides.

"Eric, I'm exhausted," she pleaded. "I'm not up to discussing this now."

"We have to," he replied. *If for no other reason than my own peace of mind.* "I need to know if you think Wayne lit that spot fire intending to harm himself."

She stared at him incredulously. "You're suggesting he committed suicide."

Eric looked down at the Persian rug.

"How could you even think such a thing?" Accusation weighted her voice. "Wayne was a churchgoer. In our faith, suicide sentences a person to Hell. He would never have done something like that. Never."

"*Ja,* well, we both know he wasn't acting like himself, Jackie." The words sounded harsh, and Eric paced to the window, staring out at the lake and the cars still parading through town.

A glimpse of a McDonald's sign through the trees tripped a thought. One of the ramifications of high cholesterol and high triglycerides was an increased risk of heart disease. A stroke — or a series of small strokes — could have triggered Wayne's forgetfulness.

"Had Wayne ever suffered a stroke?" he asked.

"No!" she answered.

Eric glanced at her. Alzheimer's, schizophrenia, senile dementia, certain types of psychosis — they were all reasons why someone might exhibit patterns of inconsistent and unexplained behavior. He wondered how Jackie would react if he started down the list.

"Let's get something straight right now," said Jackie. "I'm getting quite tired of people asking me if Wayne is all right. He's fine." She looked up, making eye contact. "Granted, he's been acting a little odd lately, but he's had a lot on his mind. His only

125

daughter is about to graduate and go off to college. He's nearing retirement and trying to figure out what to do with himself. Plus, his father's been sick."

She scooted forward and straightened a stack of coasters on the table. "Of course, Dad's been sick a long time, but things have gotten worse lately."

"What's wrong with Wayne's —"

"I'll admit, Wayne has been under a lot of stress. But he would never do anything intentionally that caused Tamara or me any pain."

Eric noticed she spoke of Wayne in the present-tense. *Denial.*

Draped in widow's black, running her finger along the smooth end of a stack of crystal coasters, she seemed lost in thought, and unaware that her husband was dead. Suddenly Eric felt like an ass.

"You're right, Jackie," he said. "We don't need to be talking about this."

Emotion — a cross between guilt and pity — flickered across her face. Her chin trembled. "Oh God, here I am lecturing you, when I know how much Wayne meant to you."

"*Ja*, well, just forget I asked." What difference did it make anyway? Wayne was dead. All that mattered now was making sure Jackie and Tamara were taken care of.

"No, you're right," she said abruptly. "We have to fight this." She stared at him now,

126

her tears gone, her eyes dry and direct. "If they blame Wayne and I end up getting sued, I could lose the pension, not to mention the bonus pay and the house. Tamara might not be able to go to college."

"Slow down, Jackie. I was asking so that I understood, not seeking ammunition to take on the National Park Service. They're my employer. The report is considered final."

"Nothing's final."

Except death.

Their eyes met.

Eric looked back out the window. "I don't see any way to fight it. The jurisdiction falls to the National Park Service law enforcement officers, and, except for the autopsy, they've completed their investigation. According to them, the evidence shows —"

The coasters tumbled, clattering onto the tabletop. "The report didn't include the autopsy?"

"Only a preliminary," said Eric. "It indicated that Wayne had fallen and struck his head. Why?"

She gathered the coasters, then stood and crossed the rug toward him. "Maybe there's something in the autopsy we can use to prove Wayne didn't start that fire. That's all we have to do, isn't it? Prove that he didn't do it, or that he had a valid reason for doing so?"

"The investigation team was thorough,

Jackie. The evidence collected proved Wayne was holding the fusee that started the fire. The NPS isn't going to reopen the case unless someone comes up with some pretty compelling evidence to refute their findings."

Jackie straightened her shoulders. "Then we will. I don't know what happened, but I refuse to believe Wayne did anything wrong." Her eyes opened wide. "What if someone framed him?"

"Like who?"

"I don't know. Maybe that Trent fellow."

Pacey Trent had needed a scapegoat, but would he have gone so far as to lay the blame on a dead man?

"Or what if Nora Frank decided she couldn't wait for Wayne's job?" Bitterness clung to Jackie's voice. Eric had thought she liked Nora.

"I seriously doubt that Nora —"

"You know as well as I do," Jackie interrupted, "that with Wayne gone, his job along with a substantial raise in pay belongs to her." Jackie sniffed. "Unless of course, she screws up."

Eric swallowed. Spit stuck in his throat. "Let me get this straight. You're suggesting someone —"

"Murdered him."

Chapter 12

Her words resonated in his soul. The rantings of a grief-stricken widow. Yet, somehow the idea seemed more palatable than suicide. Even he had allowed himself to visit the idea, the concept of foul play niggling at the back of his mind when he'd first heard that Wayne died from a blow to the head. The missing pickup and psychrometer had added fuel to the theory, then, reminded of Wayne's earlier behavior, Eric had allowed himself to be sidetracked into thinking Wayne might have wanted to kill himself.

What if his gut instinct had been right after all?

The idea that Pacey Trent had murdered Wayne was too far-fetched to consider. Trent had no need to go to such extremes to find a scapegoat. He could have pinned the blame for the fire on Nora Frank.

Unless Wayne had decided to call off the burn. If so, he would have contacted Trent, who had a vested interest in seeing the fire lit.

As for Nora, it was no secret she wanted Wayne's job. But badly enough to murder him for it?

And what about the missing truck? The fact that it had never been found indicated someone had taken it. Maybe the missing boys from the Youth Camp? The troubled teens had yet to turn up, though Search and Rescue had tracked them through the woods on the backside of Eagle Cliff Mountain. Maybe the boys had encountered Wayne while making their escape, conked him over the head, and stolen his truck.

"You'd thought of it too," said Jackie, pulling Eric back from his thoughts.

Murder.

He stood for a moment, watching a flock of pine siskins cavort at the hanging feeder, so carefree in contrast to the solemnness brought about by Wayne's death. "What did Wayne tell you he was planning when he left Friday morning?"

"I already told you, Eric. He said he wanted to test the humidity up on Eagle Cliff Mountain."

"Do you know if he mentioned it to anyone else?"

She shook her head. "I don't remember him making a phone call, but then he left early. I got up and made him coffee while he checked his pack."

"Do you know if he took a weather kit with him?"

Jackie looked at Eric blankly.

"A psychrometer," he explained. "It's a

small, flat device with two thermometers bolted to it that's attached to a metal handle by a small chain."

He made a circular motion with his wrist. A psychrometer was used in the field to determine humidity levels, and Wayne would have had one to test the humidity on the mountain. In a standard weather kit, the right-hand thermometer, called the "dry bulb," was read and the temperature recorded. The left-hand thermometer, the "wet bulb," has a cloth attached. The cloth is soaked in water, then the psychrometer is swung in a circular motion. The evaporation of the wet cloth causes a cooling effect that drops the wet bulb temperature below that of the dry bulb, and the difference in temperatures determines the level of humidity. The missing psychrometer supported the investigation team's theory that Wayne had not gone up on the mountain to test humidity levels.

"I didn't pay that much attention," said Jackie. "Why?"

"They didn't find one among his things, or anywhere on the ground."

"Which means . . . ?"

"He couldn't run any tests, or didn't plan on running any."

They looked at each other. "Or someone took it," they said in unison.

But again, why? The only possible reason was that the thermometers showed that the humidity was too low to safely light the burn.

"Maybe he left the kit in the truck," suggested Jackie.

Eric supposed it was possible. Wayne might have taken his readings down lower, then decided to hike in and . . . what? Look around some more? Or, light a fire?

A door slammed, and Tamara shuffled down the hallway to the stairs. A smaller, thinner version of her mother, her eyes were red-rimmed and nearly swollen shut from crying.

"Mom?"

"I'm right here." Turning to go to her daughter, Jackie squeezed Eric's arm. "I'm counting on you."

His chest tightened. "I promise I'll do what I can."

Eric polished off the bottle of water on the walk home. Flipping on the television, he surfed the channels and stopped on KEPC-TV when Linda Verbiscar's face filled the screen. Eric clicked off the mute, catching her words midstream.

". . . from park headquarters where we're waiting for official word on the cause of this week's fire."

A shot of the Visitor Center appeared on the screen, with the charred remains of Beaver Meadows visible in the background.

Small tendrils of smoke rose from blackened stands of sage and bitterbrush, and the soil looked like a moonscape.

"Linda," said the studio newscaster. "While we wait for the park officials, perhaps you'd like to take this opportunity to update us on the latest developments in the wake of this disaster."

"Well, Dan, as you know, one man is dead. Wayne Devlin, age fifty-four. As Rocky Mountain National Park's fire management officer, Devlin was the man responsible for this week's burn. He was discovered burned to death on Eagle Cliff Mountain late Saturday afternoon.

"It's widely thought that Devlin headed out to test the humidity levels early on the morning of the burn. One thing's for certain, he never showed up at command central. And, it now appears, he may in fact have started the fire that caused so much damage, and indeed cost him his life."

"Does that mean we should expect the Park Service to declare this an arson fire?"

"That is a possibility, Dan. My sources tell me that Wayne Devlin had, in fact, been acting strangely before he died. In digging, I learned that he has for the past year been under a neurologist's care at the University Medical Center."

Eric stared at the picture of Linda. That meant that Jackie had lied to him about

Wayne's behavior. If he'd been seeing a neurologist, she had to have known something was wrong.

"Do we know what he was being treated for, Linda?"

"Patient records are confidential, Dan, and we haven't been able to root out that information. Perhaps today's press conference will shed additional light on the situation."

In the background, there was a flurry of commotion as the Visitor Center doors opened, then closed again. No one emerged.

Verbiscar turned back to the camera. "In other developments, there is still no word on the two missing boys from the Youth Mountain Camp."

"Tell us what you know about the camp, Linda. Is my impression correct? Is this a camp for troubled youth?"

"Yes, Dan. The Youth Mountain Camp runs an innovative program designed to help teens between the ages of fifteen and eighteen who have all had some type of run-in with the law. The youth are recommended into the program by police or probation officers from throughout the greater Denver metropolitan area. By all accounts, the program has met with varying degrees of success."

"Do we know anything specific about the missing boys, Linda? For instance, do we know why they were sent to the Youth

134

Mountain Camp?"

"No, Dan. We've been unable to obtain that information. Victor Garcia, Elk Park's county sheriff, himself a former attendee of the camp, and who now helps run the facility, has been very tight-lipped. As has Bernie Crandall, Elk Park's chief of police. The one thing we do know is, the boys' names are Lewis Kennedy the third, more commonly known as Tres, and one Justin Suett. Tres resides with his parents in the Cherry Creek area, Cherry Hills Farms to be exact, and Justin comes from the Castle Pines area."

Eric rubbed his chin. Both were upscale neighborhoods. Rich boys, with too much money and too much time on their hands. Privileged kids looking for excitement, and finding trouble instead.

"Wait. It looks like people are exiting the building behind you, Linda."

"Yes, Dan." The camera zoomed in on Pacey Trent. "It appears that the fire management officer for the Intermountain Regional NPS is finally ready to make a statement. Let's hear what he has to say."

Trent's announcement was short, and to the point. Exactly what he'd told Eric it would be — a pronouncement of Wayne's guilt.

Eric climbed into his truck and headed into Elk Park as the sun dropped behind

Longs Peak and twilight settled into the valley. Rolling down the pickup's window, he rested his elbow on the sill and allowed the cool breeze to sift through his hair. The air smelled faintly of smoke, but not enough to cause alarm. The fire was out.

Turning right onto Devil's Gulch Road, he looked to see if there were any lights on at Lark's place. The carriage house stood dark behind the Drummond Hotel, and he tamped down his disappointment. Maybe she'd be back by the time he finished feeding the birds at the Raptor House rehabilitation center.

Fire or no fire, taking care of the rehab center occupants — a permanently injured eagle named Isaac, six red-tailed hawks, two golden eagles, a few kestrels, and a great horned owl — fell under Eric's job description. A volunteer at the center since it opened over sixteen years ago, he'd been assigned there permanently after William Tanager, the previous owner, had died. William's wife, Miriam, had turned the daily operations over to the Park Service. The Tanager family owned the land in trust. NPS ran the center.

There were seven buildings in all. The big barn housed the intensive care unit and offices, and all incoming and outgoing birds were processed through there. The remaining buildings were designated care units, pinpointed for separate species, or designated for

136

special services. The Nesting Compound housed burrowing owls and stood empty now. The Pygmy House sheltered the smaller owls and kestrels. The Eagles' Eyrie housed eagles. Collegiate Hall sheltered the educational birds — ones used for school programs that for a number of reasons could never be returned to the wild. In addition, there was the hospital ward, Protective Custody House, and the Freedom House, where birds took their final test flights before being released.

Accelerating up Raptor House Road, Eric relaxed, listening to the sounds of the evening. Wind whooshed past the window, and rustled the trees. In the distance he heard a common nighthawk call, *peent, peent,* as it sang its courtship song. The sounds of life. A far cry from the stifling depression of the Devlin house.

Pulling past Bird Haven, Miriam Tanager's house, Eric was surprised to see Lark's truck parked in front.

"Hey, stranger," she called from the porch.

Eric slowed. He hadn't seen her standing outside.

"Hey, yourself." Eric grinned, feeling more like a seventeen-year-old trolling for girls in downtown Lillehammer than a thirty-five-year-old park ranger on his way to work. "What's going on?"

"The EPOCH meeting." She sounded surprised, then smiled. "I take it you forgot."

He had, though the Elk Park Ornithological Chapter met every Monday night at Bird Haven. "I came to feed the birds."

Decked out in jeans and a flannel shirt, with her hair in a French braid, Lark looked like she'd stepped out of an L.L.Bean catalog. She sauntered down the stairs, and he felt his heart bump.

"Want some company?" Lark gestured at the house. "We're starting late. Some of the others can't make it before eight."

"Sure." He tried to keep the word light, and not sound too anxious.

"Are you okay?" she asked.

"*Ja*, why?"

"You look tired."

"It's been a long day."

While he pulled frozen Coturnix quail and dead mice out of the Raptor House freezer and arranged them on a microwavable platter, he told her about the mop-up and Trent's waiting for him at the bottom of the hill.

"I saw the broadcast," Lark said.

Her tone suggested disappointment. In what? The system? She bent forward and leaned her elbows on the counter. He popped the platter into the microwave. Normally he would have thawed the birds and mice by leaving them out for a couple of hours, but tonight he punched in five minutes defrost on the keypad and hit the start button.

138

"Did you go over to the Devlins'?" she asked.

"*Ja.* I figured I owed it to Jackie to give her the news in person."

"How did she take it?"

Eric shrugged. "She wants me to help her prove he didn't start the fire." Eric related the conversation in detail, right down to the accusations. "She thinks he was framed, or murdered."

"Murdered?"

"*Ja,* that's what she suggested."

"What do you think?"

Should he confess what he was thinking? If he couldn't trust Lark, who could he trust?

"I don't know. It was my initial reaction, but . . . What if he committed suicide?"

"You think he killed himself?"

"Maybe. He'd been acting strange lately. If Linda Verbiscar was right about the neurologist, maybe he knew something was wrong with him and wanted to improve the benefits to his family."

Lark scrunched up her face.

"It wouldn't be the first time someone's done that." The timer dinged, and Eric snatched the platter of quail and mice from the microwave.

"Do you think Jackie's worried about losing Wayne's pension?"

"*Ja.* You can't really blame her."

Lark shook her head in agreement. "You

know, Forest Nettleman told Dorothy Mac-Bean he's planning to sue."

Eric stabbed the meat hard with a fork. Flesh cracked beneath the pressure. "He's a jerk."

Lark puffed out a breath in what Eric took for agreement.

"He told Dorothy that he wanted to use the media exposure to make a statement."

"What kind of statement?" asked Eric, shoving the platter back in the microwave and punching in another five-minute defrost cycle.

"Apparently Forest hired Linda Verbiscar to produce an IMAX-style documentary for the Wildland Center. Some gung-ho piece on fire and its effects on avian and wildlife populations. From what Dorothy said, they share a common interest in 'educating the public on conservation needs.'" She made quote marks in the air. "Their focus is on the National Park System."

Eric bent down, facing Lark and placing his elbows opposite hers on the counter. He could feel the electricity spark between them. "What's their stand?"

"Anti-burn. Neither one of them agree with the NPS's attempt to micromanage through prescribed burning."

"I should have guessed." The timer counted down, and Eric pushed up from the counter.

"No," said Lark. She reached out and touched his arm.

"No, what?"

"They're not anti-burn, rather anti-suppression slash pro natural burn."

"In other words," said Eric "they're all for a lightning strike fire burning down the Wildland Center, just not one that's man-made."

"You've got it."

Eric checked the quail again. This time the flesh was supple, and the smell confirmed the dead mice had thawed. "Come on. It's supper time."

Chapter 13

In companionable silence, Lark opened doors while Eric dished out meals and the birds conversed, squealing and shrieking their delight at being fed. Like children in a buffet line, some dug right in with enthusiasm, while others hung back and eyed the food with suspicion.

Pitching a dead mouse to a kestrel, Eric mulled over the events of the past two days — the fire, the firestorm, Wayne's death. Animal instinct and the will to survive drove most creatures, and humans were nothing if not animals. Eric began to wonder if he'd been right in the first place.

"Lark, can you think of anyone who might have wanted Wayne dead?" he asked.

Lark fumbled the latch on the door to the peregrine mews. "Excuse me?"

"Playing the devil's advocate, who leaps to mind? Can you think of anyone who stood to gain by Wayne's death?"

Lark frowned, wrestling with the lock. "Jackie," she answered, sliding back the door.

"Okay, besides her. She's the widow, not a suspect, remember."

"Maybe, but she's a widow with great motives. She would be sitting pretty right now, if Wayne hadn't been found negligent for lighting the fire." Lark held up her hand and ticked the reasons off on her fingers, starting with her pinkie. "First there's his pension."

Eric bristled. "Now attachable for damages, and less than he brought in alive."

Lark pointed to her ring finger. "Add the death-while-on-duty pay."

"Uncollectible," said Eric. "He's been found guilty of negligence, remember?"

Lark shrugged, closed and relatched the door, then held up her hand, adding her middle finger to the count. "Third, there's the money dished out by the Benefits Act."

"Now forfeit." Eric didn't like the case Lark was building, and he felt like a traitor even considering Jackie.

"Now," said Lark. "But what about before?"

"You can't deny Jackie loved him," Eric countered.

Lark patted her chest with her finger-counting hand. "Hey, devil's advocate, re-member? I'm on your side. I agree, she loved him a lot, but you're the one who asked who I thought stood to gain. Financially, Jackie was the person who stood to gain the most."

"You're right," conceded Eric, pushing through the outer door and heading down the sidewalk toward the next building. "I did ask. I just wasn't prepared for your answer."

Lark fell in step beside him. "So, do they

know when the fire started?"

Was she trying to change the subject? Eric cocked his head. "Based on the size of the fire and the wind, the investigation team figures sometime between 8 and 10 a.m. They can't be more exact because the site was overrun by fire a second time. They think the fire Wayne set —"

"Allegedly set."

Eric smiled at her. "Allegedly . . . might have smoldered awhile before taking off." Eric's mind played over the minutes before the firestorm — finding Wayne's body, the Beaver Meadows Fire crowning the ridge, deploying the shelters. Then shaking off the memories, he glanced at Lark. "I talked to Jackie around 8 a.m., and then again just before nine. She was home."

Lark grinned. "Then she's off the hook, because she came into the Warbler around nine-thirty to buy coffee. There's no possible way she could have climbed Eagle Cliff Mountain between the time you say you talked with her and the time she showed up at the coffeehouse."

Eric stopped walking. For the second time in as many days, he wanted to kiss Lark. A happy, but extremely uncomfortable realization. The two of them had been dancing around each other for a while, but a kiss was a huge step considering how long they'd been friends. He didn't want to do anything to jeopardize their friendship, yet . . .

"What?" she asked.

He wet his lips, then shook his head. "Nothing."

Lark frowned. "So, who does that leave?"

"Trent," said Eric, moving again. "Or Nora, or the missing boys." He explained how he had it figured while Lark unlocked the door of the Protective Custody House. "Pacey Trent wanted to shed a positive light on prescribed burning, and Nora wanted Wayne's job so bad she could taste it. Wayne stood in both of their ways."

"I don't get it," said Lark, shoving back the door. Eric squeezed past her, shouldering his way through an inner door to the mews.

"It's like this," explained Eric. "Wayne was considering calling off the burn because of the fire danger. Trent was adamant the burn was going to happen. And Nora had been trying to force Wayne out for over a year. She'd been working to get him fired."

"Why?"

"Because of how strangely he'd been acting. She didn't think he was fit for duty."

"Do you think one of them could have killed him?" asked Lark.

"Could, or would?" Eric reached into the bucket, pitched the last quail to a red-tailed hawk, and watched the bird tear the meat apart. "Hungry people do desperate things."

Lark worried her lower lip. "Okay, as-

145

suming they both wanted Wayne dead, and were capable of murdering him, who had the chance?”

“Not Trent,” admitted Eric. “He was accounted for at all times. Though, he could easily have planted evidence in order to make it look like Wayne started the fire.”

“Framing someone is different than murdering them,” said Lark. “What about Nora?”

Lifting the empty bucket, Eric headed back toward the kitchen. Lark padded behind, and Eric answered her over his shoulder. “She disappeared for over an hour, right after the blowup occurred.”

“But would she have started a fire?”

“Maybe to cover up evidence.”

“Seems risky to me,” said Lark.

“*Ja*, well . . .” Eric held open the Raptor House door and waited for Lark to brush past.

“And the missing boys?” she asked.

Eric didn’t know about them. “It’s only supposition, but, suppose they stumbled upon Wayne in the woods. They might have bashed him over the head in order to steal his truck.”

“I’ll buy that.” Lark crossed the room and scootched her rear end up on the counter, while Eric rinsed the platter. “I cast my vote for the missing boys. But, again, there’s the question of the fire.”

Eric set the platter into the dishwasher, slid

in the rack, then slammed the door and leaned against the opposite counter. "What if we're looking at this all wrong? What if it wasn't someone targeting Wayne, but someone Wayne stumbled upon who bashed him in the head? Maybe Wayne surprised someone setting a fire?"

Lark toyed with the end of her braid. "Who?"

"The missing boys? They might have been building a campfire. Or, how about Nettleman?"

"Forest?" She sounded incredulous.

"Why not? He's got a reputation for taking things to the extreme. Weren't you the one who said he was against selective burning?"

"Yeah, but setting a forest fire to prove you're anti-burn seems a bit over the top."

"If the shoe fits," said Eric, leaning back against the counter. "You can't tell me you doubt he's capable of extreme behavior. The American public didn't. You didn't see them reelecting him to Congress."

"So he has a history."

"He's been known to do things for the cause," said Eric. Dousing a rag in hot water, he started wiping down the microwave. "Maybe this time he was hoping to prove his theory to the general public."

"Then he may have succeeded." Lark's fingers inched up the weave of her braid. "Right now the general Elk Park population isn't ex-

147

actly embracing the NPS burn policy. Of course, if we're going on the-killer-surprised-Wayne-in-the-woods theory, there could be any number of suspects. Campers, hikers . . .''

"Linda Verbiscar," offered Eric.

"Why her?"

"She was very anxious for fire footage. The moment the first blowup occurred, she and her cameraman bolted toward Eagle Cliff Mountain."

"Did they get to the fire line?"

"I don't think so." Eric made a mental note to ask Pacey Trent. "But she was desperate for close-up footage."

"Enough to create her own?"

Eric recalled Linda's grilling, how she had twisted his words, and her tenacity at the press conference regarding Wayne. "She's a tough bird."

"Tough enough to kill someone?"

"That's the real question, isn't it?" Eric hung the rag on the spigot, and Lark slid off the counter.

"If we're looking at all the possibles, there's also Gene Paxton," she said.

Eric cocked his head.

"Rumor has it the guy used chintzy building materials. He didn't have as much invested in Shangri-la as everyone thinks, but he's reported substantial investments and stands to make a ton of money when the insurance pays off. Not to mention the amounts he'll collect from the Park Service and Wayne Devlin's estate."

Insurance fraud?

Eric flipped out the light. Placing his hand on the small of Lark's back, he ushered her toward the door. "I wonder what the first thing to do is."

"Check everyone's alibis," said Lark with the voice of experience. "We know Jackie and Trent are out. They're accounted for at the time of the murder."

Eric slid the Raptor House door shut. "Do you think Dorothy can vouch for Nettleman?"

Lark shook her head. "She and Cecilia were waiting for me at the house when I came off the fire. I remember Dorothy saying Forest had left the Wildland Center an hour before she received the evacuation order."

"Which means Forest Nettleman had plenty of time to climb Eagle Cliff Mountain." Eric yanked hard on the lock, then steered Lark toward Bird Haven. "Do you know, does Nettleman own an ATV?"

The Elk Park Ornithological Chapter meeting hadn't formally convened by the time Lark and Eric arrived. The usual attendees — Miriam Tanager, Forest Nettleman, Harry, Dorothy, Cecilia, Andrew and Opal Henderson from the valley, and Gertie Tanager — along with a handful of irregulars had gathered in the living room at Bird Haven. Rachel Stanhope was the only regular missing, having returned to New York in the fall. Overhead, a chandelier constructed of tangled antlers, electric wires, and candlelike lightbulbs cast a pale light over the crowd. Warm lamplight reflected off leaded glass windows, and burnished floors. A soft, leather, burgundy-colored couch anchored the room, along with scattered rugs and a moss rock fireplace.

Forest Nettleman perched on the hearth. Tall and gangly, he straightened when he saw Eric. "Well, speak of the devil."

Eric wondered if he meant it literally.

"Come over here a minute, Eric. Perhaps you can settle something." Nettleman made a circular motion with his hand.

Eric groaned.

Lark elbowed him in the stomach. "Be nice."

"Sure," he wheezed, sidestepping a second blow.

Leaving her to talk with Miriam, he crossed the living room toward Nettleman and Andrew Henderson. Nettleman extended his right hand but didn't stand. Henderson — a super-sized man with a super-sized appetite and a scraggly goatee — sat on the couch. He stuffed a cracker into his mouth, and waved.

"We're in the midst of a debate," explained Nettleman, gesturing between himself and Henderson. "As you no doubt know, I'm a staunch opponent of prescribed burning. I have been from the start. Andy, here, disagrees with me."

Henderson's face reddened. "The name is Andrew, if you don't mind," he said, forcing his words around the hors d'oeuvres in his mouth.

"Right," conceded Nettleman, acting like he'd just remembered. Never mind that he'd known Henderson for years.

"Anyway," he continued. "From what I hear via the grapevine, Eric, you and I were on the same side. You were against the burn, too."

"On this one, *ja*," admitted Eric.

"I told you." Nettleman beamed at Henderson, then focused his piercing blue eyes on Eric. "Do you mind telling us why?"

Eric chafed under the questioning. He didn't like being played, and he suspected Nettleman was setting him up. "Is there a prize for the right answer?"

Henderson choked on the cracker. Nettleman frowned.

Eric waited another beat, then said, "In my opinion? The fire danger was too high."

"And you were right," said Nettleman.

A small consolation, thought Eric. "I was also concerned about the number of breeding

151

birds in the area," he said. "A lot of towhees and warblers have moved in. They were nesting, and I hated to see them driven out."

"Very admirable," concurred Nettleman. "Not even someone as pro-burn as Henderson could dispute that logic."

Henderson wiped his mouth on a napkin and started to speak, when Nettleman bulldozed over him.

"Humidity and avian factors not withstanding, you support the burns, Eric." Nettleman rested his elbows on his knees. "I'd like to know why."

Swinging his leg up along the back of the sofa, Eric sat down. "Honestly, I think the fire management policy speaks for itself. Prescribed burning accomplishes one main thing. It eliminates the buildup of fuels and decreases the danger for catastrophic wildfire."

"Unless," pointed out Nettleman, "it's the burn itself that becomes the catastrophe."

"*Ja*," said Eric. "There is that." He picked at a loose thread of stitching on the couch. "It's too bad what happened. I'm sorry for the loss."

"Too bad?" Nettleman choked out a laugh. "Your 'controlled burn' was a total disaster. And one, I might add, the NPS owes restitution for. Let me say, once the federal boys get a copy of my bill, they won't be so eager to rubber stamp the prescriptions. In fact at my urging, the governor has already declared

152

a moratorium on burning, and I think you'll see more repercussions as time goes on."

Only, it wasn't "the federal boys" who were going to pay up. It was Wayne Devlin's estate that owed.

"Accidental destruction of private property aside," said Nettleman. "It's a bad idea to play God, Eric."

"I wouldn't say we go that far, Forest."

Henderson grunted in support.

"No?" Nettleman stared with incredulity at the two men. "I beg you to take a closer look at the theory, gentlemen. According to popular belief, prescribed burning replicates the natural fire patterns, reintroducing fire into the ecosystem, correct?"

"You've got that much right," said Henderson, sliding forward to the edge of the couch. "After almost a hundred years of fire suppression, our forests are choking to death in undergrowth. Fire will fix that."

"Will it? How? Burning in May doesn't replicate natural fire," argued Nettleman, warming to the subject as he drew an audience from the other birders. "For instance, studies have proven that certain plants flower at certain times. Isn't it safe then to assume that fire impacts the growing season?"

Several people nodded and moved in closer.

"Then let's take it a step further," said Nettleman. "In the state of Colorado, our natural fire season is between late June and early August, right? But when do we burn? April. May. Late fall. Why? So we can control the fire." He turned to Eric. "Admit it."

"What's your point, Forest?"

"My point is, prescribed burns take place within a time frame limited to the dormant season, and accomplishes, what? The removal of duff, litter, and the grasses — the coverings of the forest floor. Have you never considered that by burning at this time of the year, we're also altering the basic composition of our forests and open lands?"

Eric glanced at the faces of his friends. "You cited studies, Forest. The studies don't prove that. In fact, a majority suggest fire is of benefit to the land."

"But you can't deny that the timing of a burn isn't critical to responsible ecosystem management. Or that a fire in the traditional season isn't best." Nettleman settled back against the side of the moss rock fireplace. "Tell them, Eric. Tell them about the studies." Nettleman turned to the others. "I'm telling you, folks. By burning when we do, we may actually be altering the natural vegetative state of our forests and encouraging the growth of nonnative plants while suppressing the ability of the native plants to grow."

Eric rose to his feet, taking the floor. "I'll admit, there have been some studies." He held up his hand to quiet the birders. "But they were studies based in Florida. We've seen no signs of that happening here. The biggest impact we've observed is the change made by fire on the immediate habitat."

"What kind of changes are we talking about, Eric?" prompted Henderson.

"That depends on the intensity of the fire. The goal is to have a low-intensity fire that reduces the fuel loads but doesn't impact the environment long term."

"What happens if it's a high-intensity fire?" asked Dorothy MacBean, joining the conversation and sidling up next to Forest Nettleman.

"A high-intensity fire burns in the crown, in the tops of the trees," explained Eric. "It causes severe damage to the forests, killing the trees, and destroying the nesting habitat and food supply for a large number of birds."

"But don't certain birds thrive on fire?" asked Henderson, displaying his allegiance to Eric by facing off Dorothy MacBean.

"Not in the long run," answered Nettleman. "There's an initial increase in bird count. Raptors move in to feed on the small animals left without cover. Woodpeckers dine on the exposed bugs. But overall, the studies show a decline in the number of birds for a twenty- to twenty-five-year period."

"Oh my," said Cecilia.

"Not with a low-intensity burn. Then the

damage is negligible," said Eric. "In a year or so, you'd never even know there'd been a burn."

Eric found it ironic he was using Nora's logic — an argument he'd rejected a few days ago — to convince the birders to accept RMNP's fire management policies. Maybe he wasn't being honest with himself.

"So, Forest, tell us what you propose," said Dorothy.

"Nothing." Nettleman preened beneath the shocked stares of his listeners. "I propose that we stop lighting fires and that we let natural wildfires burn themselves out. No suppression. No intervention. No participation in any way. It's time we allow Mother Nature to plot her own course."

"What about when a fire roars into town?" demanded Henderson. "Or when it's your house, or the Wildland Center burning down? Surely you don't think we should just stand by and roast weenies on the carnage."

"That's exactly what I'm advocating. If a structure is in the path, it's meant to burn."

"Okay, everybody, listen up," said Miriam, banging her fist on the bar. "I'd like to call this meeting to order."

Eric hesitated, then turned to face Miriam. Nettleman leaned forward.

"On a final note," he said quietly. "This fire may be all it takes for me to convince the National Park Service boys that I'm right.

Somewhat of a disguised blessing, in more ways than one."

Eric stiffened.

Lark, who had sidled up next to Eric when Miriam called the meeting to order, leaned over and whispered, "Is everything okay?"

"*Jeg foler ugler I mosen,*" he answered.

Lark looked puzzled.

"I sense owls in the moss," Eric translated. "In English, something feels wrong."

Chapter 14

Miriam quickly dispensed with the preliminaries and moved onto old business — an update on the protocol for reporting rare bird sightings, a report from the field trip committee on upcoming events, a standing request for newsletter articles, and the scheduling of a cleanup day along the Paris Mills Nature Trail.

"Now, does anyone have any new business?" she asked.

"I do," said Eric. He wasn't anxious to make his request in the wake of the earlier conversation with Forest, but maybe it would work to his advantage. Miriam gestured for him to take the floor, and he moved to where he could face the gathering.

"I'm sure all of you know by now that the recent fire affected over nine-thousand acres," he said. "Mostly Park Service land, but some privately owned property, too."

Cecilia reached out to clutch Dorothy's arm, while the other bird watchers whispered among themselves. Eric raised his voice above the buzz. "Beaver Meadows was the primary park habitat for the green-tailed towhee and Virginia's warbler. The meadows area was decimated. We also lost some of the forested habitat for three-toed woodpeckers."

The buzz increased, and Miriam rapped on the bar. "Let him finish."

Gertie Tanager, Miriam's step-daughter, glanced at her watch, then glared at the others. "You know, some of us have to work tomorrow."

Eric continued. "For the next few months —"

"Years," interjected Lark.

"Whatever," said Gertie.

"Years," Eric amended. "The thing is, the NPS needs volunteers. It's my job to pinpoint the location of plants surviving in the burned-out areas and to document the return of wildlife." He paused, and scanned the faces of his friends. "I'm sure you realize, this type of study is essential to understanding the effects of fire on avian populations and habitats. I am hoping I can count on EPOCH to supply some manpower."

Henderson scratched his goatee. "How many hours a day do you need?"

"Whatever you can give," answered Eric. "Ideally we'd like to have someone, or a number of someones, observe a designated area during a specific time every day."

Nettleman raised his hand. "Excuse me. Exactly what is your primary objective?" he asked. "What's the goal of the observation?"

"We need to do two things. One, gauge the

amount of new growth versus the amount of food the elk are consuming. And, two, determine the impact of prescribed burning on various bird and animal species."

"To prove what?" asked Nettleman, rolling his eyes. "That prescribed burns adversely affect the wildlife?"

Eric bristled. "I believe we've covered this ground, Forest. But if you're asking me on a personal level what I care about most, it's the effect of the burn on the green-tailed towhee."

"You want my guess?" Nettleman turned from Eric and addressed the group. "It's negative."

Eric's face heated up. "We're not interested in guesses, Forest. We're interested in facts. The NPS needs to document the effect so we can factor the evidence into future burn plans."

"That sounds easy enough," Lark interjected. "Do we need to make a motion?"

Miriam shook her head. "I encourage all of you to participate. Eric will set up a volunteer schedule and post it at the Raptor House. Those interested in helping out should stop by there and sign up for available times."

"Thanks," said Eric, heading back to his seat.

"Excuse me," said Nettleman, clearing his throat. "What I don't understand is why the

National Park Service bothers to use people?"

Eric halted midway across the Persian carpet.

"Would you care to explain that, Forest?" asked Miriam.

"Well, people get sick, don't show up, and miss seeing or identifying things. Human observation is fallible. That's why the Wildland Center uses motion-sensor video cameras for all of its studies. We've found using cameras to be much more accurate and dependable."

"And expensive," Eric remarked.

"True," agreed Nettleman. "But it only takes one or two digital videocams mounted in strategic locations to cover most sites. They're worth their weight in gold."

"And people aren't?" asked Eric. "Then who evaluates the videotape?"

Lark muffled a laugh behind her collar, her shoulders shaking. Nettleman looked flustered.

Eric raised an eyebrow. "Thanks for the suggestion, Forest. I'll keep it in mind." He walked over to where Lark was standing, then turned back. "Hey, you don't happen to have any videocameras you'd be willing to lend the Park Service, do you?"

Miriam rapped her knuckles on the bar. "This meeting is adjourned."

The group dispersed quickly. Eric drove home, pulling into his driveway by eleven o'clock. His headlamps skimmed the outside wall of the small cabin, and he flicked them off, killing the engine and soaking in the night.

A sliver of moon shone overhead, casting enough light to highlight the rim of the mountain range extending to the north and etch the outlines of the trees at the edge of the horizon. In the distance, a great horned owl hooted, and a rabbit or other small animal rustled the bushes nearby. Overhead, the stars glittered against a black-purple sky.

He climbed out of the truck and crunched across the gravel to the door, aware of the smoky smell that lingered in the air, of the cool breeze blowing out of the west, and of the feeling of contentment draping his shoulders.

The telephone's voice mail light broke the spell, pulsing with an even beat from the corner of the living room. Eric felt his heart jump into a quickened rhythm in the dark.

Crossing the room, he punched on the speakerphone, keyed in his access numbers, and listened.

"You have one unheard message," said the prerecorded voice. "First message, received today at 10:51 p.m."

He'd just missed the call.

"Hello? Eric? Linda Verbiscar. I need to talk with you as soon as possible. I've come across something I think you'll want to see.

162

I'm at nine-seven-zero, five-five-five, six-seven-three-zero. It doesn't matter how late."

Eric replayed the message, wondering what she wanted. They'd met only once, at the turnaround, just after the blowup on the Beaver Meadows fire. As memory served, she'd made him look like an ass on KEPC News at Noon.

"I've come across something I think you'll want to see," her voice repeated.

The kitchen clock read just after the hour.

"It doesn't matter how late."

What the heck. She had just called.

Eric punched in her number, and was surprised when she picked up. He'd been expecting to get her office voice mail, but instead, her groggy voice crossed the line.

"Sorry," he said. "I guess I woke you."

"It's okay. I'd just gone to bed," she answered, her voice clearing. "It's Eric, right?"

"*Ja.*"

"I'm glad you called. I hit the jackpot." She sounded excited. He waited for her to go on.

"I have a piece of evidence that proves Wayne Devlin didn't set that fire." She paused, and Eric found himself holding his breath.

"What type of evidence?" he demanded.

"Video."

"You have footage?" He flashed on Nettleman's comments regarding the videocams,

163

and wondered if the clip came from a Wildland Center camera, or from something she and Charlie had taped on location. Adrenaline flooded his veins. "What's on the video? Does it show Wayne being murdered?"

"No. But it shows enough to pinpoint a possible murderer."

"Have you called Vic Garcia?" asked Eric, pacing the length of the phone cord, then pivoting. "Or Bernie Crandall?"

"Are you kidding? And let them confiscate the tape?" She lowered her voice, like she was afraid of being overheard. "Look, Eric, if you tell either of them about this, I'll deny I have anything."

A stab of fear raised the hairs on his neck. "Ms. Verbiscar, if you have evidence of a crime that the authorities should see, you need to turn it in."

"No frickin' way. I've waited years to be able to break a story like this." Her voice gushed out in breathless bursts. "You know the fire film for the Wildland Center? That was supposed to be my big break. With the center burned to the ground, we both know that deal's toast. But this story, it practically guarantees me a Colorado Broadcasters Association Award. Maybe even a national credit. No way I'm blowing my chance at the networks so some small-town police officer can make his case."

"Why did you call me?" He had reached the end of the cord again.

"Because to do this right, I need an interview." Her voice honeyed. "You know, Eric, you come off well on screen. You're tall, good looking, and you have great manners. 'Ms. Verbiscar.' But most important, you wear the NPS uniform. I want your reaction to the film on camera."

In violation of how many laws? thought Eric. As a park ranger, he had a responsibility to notify the proper authorities of any evidence pertaining to a crime committed in the park. Plus Nora had issued a gag order. Only official spokespersons were allowed to speak to the press. Not to mention what Verbiscar had done to him the last time she'd captured him on tape.

"What's on the video?" he asked for the second time.

"Grant me the interview and you'll find out."

"I'd be jeopardizing my job." He felt suddenly antsy. "I'm going to hang up now."

She exhaled softly, like she was smoking a cigarette. "You know, you're not the only one I've asked for an interview."

"So there are others who know about the tape?" Eric shifted his weight from foot to foot. "Who?"

"A couple of people. At least one person you know." She paused while her words sank in. "I can do this without you, Eric. If you're not interested, forget we had this conversation. But do stay tuned."

"Wait!" he said, afraid she'd hung up. If the video showed Wayne's murder, how could he refuse? "Tell me where you're staying. I'll come over, and we can discuss it in person."

He heard her fumbling with something in the background, then a clang.

"Ms. Verbiscar?"

"Hold on. I knocked the clock over. What time is it anyway? Good Lord! It's late."

"You said to call."

"Yeah, but I'm on the air at five. The station slotted me early so I could cover the funeral tomorrow. Any chance we could meet in the morning instead of tonight?"

Eric glanced at the wall calendar. He was scheduled to pick Jackie up early. She wanted to be at the church to arrange the flowers. "I could meet you at eight-thirty."

"I won't be finished yet." She expelled another slow breath. "How about after the services?"

He shook his head, then realized she couldn't see him over the phone lines. "There's the luncheon," he said. "But it should be over by two."

"Then let's meet after that. Say around three."

"Where?" Eric snatched up a pen.

"I've rented a little cabin at the Inn on 34,

off of Big Thompson Avenue. Just a little ways down the canyon on the left. Cabin G."

"I'll be there."

Eric cradled the phone. The red charge light blinked on. The room was still. Then, from outside, came a rabbit's scream.

Chapter 15

Funerals are the living's tribute to the dead. Lark had attended three — Will Tanager's, for Miriam; Esther Mills's, because she had to; and this one because Eric had asked her to come. She'd hated them all.

"Are you okay?" asked Eric, ushering her up the front walk of the Devlins' home.

"Fine." In truth, she was more worried about him. He looked uncomfortable in his black suit; and, like a kid in a school uniform, he kept tugging at the collar of his starched, white shirt.

The morning had been hard on him. Jackie had asked him to give the eulogy, then sit with her at the cemetery. The strain had taken its toll. Sorrow cut lines deep into his face, making him look drawn and tired. Lark wished they could just go home. Instead, they trailed behind the steady stream of people that poured through the front door of the Devlins' house. Stepping across the threshold, Lark braced herself for another exchange of murmured condolences.

Jackie greeted them in the hall. Dressed Jackie Kennedy-style in a tailored black suit with a veiled pillbox hat, she looked the part of the grieving widow. Her pale blond hair cupped her jaw, softening the lines of her chin. Clear, bright eyes peered out through the black gauze of her designer hat.

"Lark, I'm so glad you came." Jackie kissed air at the side of Lark's cheeks, then latched onto Eric's arm and pulled him toward the kitchen. "You don't mind if I borrow him for a minute, do you?"

"Of course . . . not," said Lark. Was that a smile she detected out of Eric?

"I'll come find you in a minute," he said.

"Take your time." Lark waved him off, then wandered toward the living room. Everywhere in the house, flower arrangements in riotous colors edged out the people. Tiger lilies from Wayne's sister Beatrice guarded the doorway; irises from a cousin in Louisiana graced the hall; and a vase full of chrysanthemums adorned a pedestal near the stairs. The only live plant — condolences from the Rocky Mountain National Park Service staff — drooped in a corner near the door, like an errant child in time-out.

A large number of NPS employees had shown up for the funeral, but neither Nora Frank nor Pacey Trent were in attendance. Understandable, considering their stance on Wayne's culpability for the Eagle Cliff Fire. Showing up would have been in poor taste.

Cards tagged the flower displays, and Lark took her time browsing the messages.

So sorry for your loss, Gil Arquette, Esq.
He will be missed, The Friends of the Library.
In Fond Remembrance, Dr. Semper.

The largest arrangement was a mixture of greens and daisies marked, *I love you, Daddy.*

Tears flooded Lark's eyes.

"Need a Kleenex?"

Lark reached for a tissue and looked up to see Tamara Devlin holding the box.

"Thanks," said Lark.

"No problem." Tamara shrugged a thin shoulder. Barely eighteen, she had the same petite frame and pale blond hair as her mother. She wore no makeup, and her red-rimmed eyes made it clear she'd been crying. At the moment, however, she appeared very calm.

"How are you holding up?" ventured Lark.

"Fine." Tamara dropped the tissue box on the coffee table. Plopping down on the white-leather couch, she crossed bare legs, her skin sallow against the hem of her black skirt. "The drugs help. I just wish all these people would get out of our house."

"I'll bet you do."

Lark wondered whether the drugs Tamara referred to had been prescribed, or were more of the garden variety. "These things don't usually last very long," she offered. "People come to pay their respects, then they leave."

"People come to eat, drink, and tell stupid jokes," said Tamara. She folded her arms across her chest and wet the inside of her upper lip with her tongue.

Cotton mouth.

"The worst is the stupid media." Tamara reached for a can of Coke sitting on the end table. "That Linda Verbiscar person is a viper. Thank God Mama finally had Sheriff Garcia throw her out."

Lark grinned. "I would have paid to see that."

"The witch made a real scene. Man, was she hot." Tamara rolled her eyes. "They ought to run a tape of that on the Five O'clock News." She took a swig of the Coke, then banged down the can, sloshing sticky liquid across a *Martha Stewart Living* magazine. "Crap, look who's here."

Lark followed the direction of Tamara's gaze and spotted Gene Paxton and Forest Nettleman entering the room.

Before Lark realized what was happening, Tamara stood up and pointed a bony finger at the two men. "You," she intoned in a frosty voice. "Both of you. Get out."

The room fell silent.

"Don't pretend you don't hear me. You know I'm talking to you," shrieked Tamara. "I want you to leave. Get out. Now!"

Someone coughed.

Lark placed a hand on Tamara's arm. "Maybe you should sit down."

"No."

"Tamara!" Jackie Devlin stepped into the doorway behind the two men. She waggled a finger at her daughter, pasting on a thin smile. "Where are your manners, young lady? These two gentlemen came here to pay their respects to your father. Surely you can show some courtesy."

"Gentlemen?" Tamara snorted. "How about bloodsuckers? Have you forgotten about the lawsuits already, Mother? But, then, maybe they don't matter to you. It's not your college tuition being siphoned away." Tamara shrugged off Lark's hand. "All I can say is, maybe you're willing to hang out with scum, but I'm not."

"Tamara, please. Stop making a scene." Jackie's tone forbade defiance. Tamara glared at her mother, then flounced out of the room.

"Honey, please." Jackie reached for her daughter, but Tamara brushed past and disappeared into the hall. Jackie pursed her lips, smoothed her dress, then said, "You'll have to forgive her. She's had a difficult time."

Murmurs of understanding filtered through the room.

"You're all so kind," said Jackie, wringing her hands.

Suddenly Eric appeared, resting his hand on the widow's shoulders. "Did I miss something?"

Jackie shook her head.

"*Vell* then, dinner is served."

The mourners closed ranks and filed toward the dining room. Lark hung back and joined the other EPOCH members, who brought up the rear.

Dorothy stood behind Lark, making a tsking sound and shaking her head. "Can you believe the way Tamara behaved? If that were my daughter —"

"Well she's not," interrupted Cecilia, glaring at her sister. "For Heaven's sake, Dottie, the girl just lost her father."

"Still, she had no business yelling at Forest."

Lark inched along watching Forest Nettleman work the room, with the sisters bickering absently in the background. He was always the politician, thought Lark. Always on, pumping a hand here, clapping a shoulder there. Too bad there weren't any babies around to kiss.

Gene Paxton, on the other hand, hung back, skirting the edges of the room. He flirted with the corners, like a wallflower afraid of being noticed. Was he embarrassed to be there, or simply trying to maintain a low profile?

It was odd the two men had come. Odder still that Jackie didn't seem to mind.

In front of Lark, the buffet table stretched the length of the dining room, sagging under the weight of the pot luck. Platters heaped with ham, turkey, and roast beef ladened one end, followed by bowls filled with rolls and a variety of salads. Casserole dishes heaped with all sorts of pasta and potatoes came next, then beverages. Against the far wall, a sidebar was buried under a mound of high-calorie desserts.

Lark groaned in sympathy with the furniture, then did her part to relieve their burden. Picking up a paper plate, some plastic flatware, and a napkin, she generously sampled the offerings.

Somewhere between the bean salad and marshmallowed fruit, Eric caught up to her in line.

"There you are," he said, his hands cupping her waist, his deep voice stirring a flood of warm pleasure that welled up from her belly.

"Hey, no butting," said Gertie Tanager.

"Sshhh!" whispered Cecilia, poking Gertie in the ribs. "Can't you see he wants to be beside Lark?"

Eric ducked his head, keeping his voice low. "I've got some good news."

"What?" Lark asked, heaping a spoonful of mustard potato salad onto her plate. His breath stirred her hair, making her shiver.

"Nora just paged me. They found Wayne's missing pickup."

Lark's head snapped up, bashing Eric in the nose.

"Oh dear," said Cecilia. "What happened? Are you all right?"

Eric nodded, covering his nose with a napkin. A spot of red blood seeped between his fingers.

"I'm sorry. And you're not all right. You're bleeding," cried Lark, mortified. Grace was not her middle name, hence two broken ankles in one year and now Eric's nose.

"Here, let me help," said Dorothy, reaching into her glass of lemonade and pulling out an ice cube. "Tip your head back."

Eric blocked Dorothy's hand. "I'm fine."

Everyone gathered around the table stared.

"Hold on," said Gertie, bubbling with excitement. "Back up the truck. Didn't he just say they found the missing boys?"

"No," said Dorothy. "He said they found Wayne's pickup. There's a difference."

"They found Wayne's truck? Where?" demanded Gene Paxton.

"They found the truck," someone whispered, spreading the word.

Lark could tell by Eric's expression that he didn't like being grilled.

"Okay, everyone," she said. "Back off. Can't you see the man's bleeding?" Setting down her plate, she steered him out of the dining room. Several people followed.

"Give him some space," she ordered.

Lark pushed Eric ahead of her, then into the tiny bathroom at the end of the hall.

175

Slamming the door in Gertie's face, she turned on the cold water. "Here, let me help. I'm so sorry."

"I'm fine." Eric tipped his head back and shoved a wad of toilet paper into his nose.

The sight of blood made Lark feel queasy, and she moved away from the sink, sitting down on the closed toilet seat. "So, where'd they find it?"

Eric removed the bloody wad of toilet paper from his nose and pitched it into the trash. "Parked in a student lot on the Colorado State University campus," he said, craning his neck in order to check the bleeding in the mirror. "Nora didn't give me any more details, but she wants me to ride down to Fort Collins with Vic and drive it back."

"When?"

"Now." Eric splashed water on his face, then used the hand towel to dry off. "I told him to pick me up at home in half an hour."

"Do they think those boys took it?"

"Vic didn't say, and neither did Nora." Eric rehung the hand towel on the holder and stuffed his hands in the pockets of his trousers. "Do you think you could get a ride back to the Drummond? I need to get home and change, and make a phone call before I leave."

"You can drop me off." Lark hoped she didn't sound too eager. The truth was, she wanted out of there.

"But you haven't eaten yet."

"That's okay. I'll grab something at home."

"Okay, then." He opened the door and gestured for her to go first, but they were blocked by a mob standing outside the door.

Lark grimaced. Since when was a bloody nose or two people in a bathroom a spectator sport?

"They're saying the sheriff found Wayne's truck," said Jackie. "Is it true?"

Lark slipped to the side. Eric's eyes crinkled at the corners, and he ran his hand through his hair. "*Ja*, they found it."

Jackie's face crumpled. For a moment, Lark thought she would cry, but no tears came.

"Nobody knows anything yet," said Eric. "I'm going with Vic to pick it up. I'll let you know what we find out." He reached for Lark's hand, but Jackie stepped between them.

"Do you promise you'll call?" she said.

Eric gripped her shoulders. "I promise. Now, do me a favor?"

Jackie nodded.

"Try not to worry."

Chapter 16

Linda Verbiscar had been ejected from the funeral reception, but she hadn't gone home.

Eric dialed her room number for the third time and listened to the phone ring. He'd left her an earlier message, apologizing for not being able to be there as planned, and promising to stop by on his way up from Fort Collins. But he wanted to talk to her personally. He wanted some reassurance that she wouldn't deny him access to the film.

The crunch of tires on gravel signaled Vic Garcia's arrival, and Eric hung up the phone.

Vic laid on the horn. "Hey there, son," he shouted. "Are you ready to go?"

Eric nodded, wondering if Vic called men "son" like some waitresses called people "honey." Eric would lay odds the tag wasn't exclusive to him.

Jumping into the passenger seat, he belted himself in and took stock of his surroundings. There was no doubt that the orange and black cruiser had seen better days. A 1996 Chevy Caprice, the cloth seats were worn, the carpets matted and thin. A vintage radio spewed Country Western music from the console, while a state band radio hissed accompaniment from the center floorboard.

Eric gestured toward a cracked shotgun holder on the floor, and Vic answered before the question was formed.

"I quit carrying it about a year ago," he announced. He didn't expound, and Eric decided not to probe.

Traffic was stop-and-go through town, signaling the onset of summer. It was a relief when Vic veered left onto U.S. 34, leaving behind the steady stream of cars headed for Denver on U.S. 36.

Eric watched for the Inn on 34. Verbiscar had said it was on the left on Big Thompson Avenue. Sure enough, within a quarter mile, he spotted the two-story motel. It clung to a flat piece of ground high above the river, horseshoed around a square pool and surrounded on all sides by miniature cabins. Two cars were parked in front of the motel office, but there were no cars in front of any of the cabins, and no people in sight. His hunch had been right. She hadn't gone home.

"Don't see her?" asked Vic.

Eric tilted his head. "How did you know I was looking for someone?"

"Just a hunch." Vic goosed the 5.7-liter, V-8 engine, and the Caprice hurtled into the canyon. "If you want my guess, she got wind of the truck's recovery. Hell, she's probably halfway to Fort Collins by now."

If he was right, she would beat them there, no matter how fast Vic chose to drive.

Eric glanced out at the canyon walls rising on either side of them. For the next thirty miles, there was only enough room between them for a river, a two-lane highway, and an occasional building. He felt squeezed in.

"Who do you think took the truck?" he asked.

"It was the boys," Vic admitted. Regret hollowed his voice. "The policeman who called in the vehicle report said there appeared to be two backpacks on the floor of the cab, along with an opened box of fusees."

That puzzled Eric. "Why leave their stuff behind?"

"Good question. Unless they're planning to come back."

Eric reached for the dashboard. "Why not stake it out, then? Catch the boys?"

Vic's hands tightened on the wheel. "We did. The Fort Collins police officer kept an eye out until Deputy Brill was in place, but your boss kiboshed the whole thing. She wants the vehicle recovered. I tried convincing her, but she insists. At this point, my hands are tied."

Eric wondered why Nora wouldn't cooperate. Maybe she was afraid catching the boys would cast doubt on the NPS hard line accusing Wayne of starting the fire. Considering her desire to have Wayne's job, that would make sense. Her aspirations for permanent placement in his vacated position might be thwarted if it was discovered she'd helped fabricate Wayne's culpability in the Eagle Cliff Fire.

"Did you ever learn anything about the missing boys?" Eric asked.

Vic tugged his seat belt tighter and settled himself deeper in his seat. "A little. I was right about Suett."

"Which one was he?" Eric tried remembering the photograph of the two boys. One was fair-haired, the other dark. If Eric remembered correctly, the blond was the scruffier-looking of the two.

"Suett's the dark-haired one. Your clean-cut, all-American, typical 'kid next door who cuts the grass'-type."

"He's the one you pegged as trouble," recalled Eric.

"That's the one." Vic swung the car around a sharp corner, and Eric braced himself against the door.

"Tres looks more like a felon," continued Vic. "But he's the quiet type. A follower. Suett's the one with problems. Big problems." Vic turned the car in the other direction. "He's a fire starter."

"An arsonist?" Eric shifted his weight, watching the road and anticipating the curves.

"Yep."

Their conversation stopped while Vic negotiated a series of hairpin turns. The car hugged the turns, snaking through the canyon carved by years of river wash. On all sides, steep slopes jutted toward the sky in craggy ridges, and high on the right, a herd of bighorn sheep graced the rock outcroppings.

The road straightened out, and the canyon widened. A few houses sprung up along the river's edge, and Eric reinitiated the conversation. "Is that why Suett was at the Youth Camp? Because he'd been caught lighting fires?"

"He was there on the recommendation of a police officer. Every kid there has to be referred. Usually, and definitely in Suett's case, it is a last-ditch effort to save the kid. The boy has quite a history." Vic shook his head and downshifted the Caprice as the canyon narrowed again.

"At age five," said Vic, "he was caught torturing the family cat, a long-haired Persian named Prudence. He'd set it on fire with his dad's butane lighter."

Eric scowled. "Did the cat live?"

Vic shrugged. "I don't know, but six years later, a week before Christmas, the family home burned down. Seems he and his cousin Leon were playing with matches. They set the tree on fire. Leon suffered third-degree burns over most of his body. He died two weeks later."

Eric calculated the years. "Suett was eleven at the time."

"Right. And he's fifteen now." Vic's knuckles turned white on the wheel. "Leon, the cousin, lived to be nine."

"Anything else happen?"

"Not that anyone knows of. Suett's been in and out of juvenile detention and foster care ever since. He's sort of an Eddie Haskell-type, a real charmer. From the report, I gathered he'd just recently moved back into his parents' home in Castle Pines."

Eric whistled. "That's a pretty upscale community."

"Nobody ever claimed crime rested solely with the underprivileged class," snapped Vic.

Eric figured he deserved the rebuff, if only because the comment sounded classist. "I didn't mean —"

His statement was cut short as Vic yanked the steering wheel, and the car lurched toward the river.

A huge rock lay in the middle of the road, forcing Vic to swerve the car hard to the right. The tires squealed on the asphalt, and the front bumper clipped the boulder, sending the car into a slide.

Vic overcorrected, and the tires spun on the soft shoulder, causing gravel to skitter onto the road.

Eric felt the car sway from side to side. The motion reminded him of schussing through a slalom course, the shifting of weight from one side to the other. A symphony of rhythm, until you caught an edge.

The tires finally grabbed on the road, and the rocking motion ceased. Vic braked, and the car slowed. Eric loosened his grip on the chicken bar. "Just a whiffle," he said. "It could have been worse."

"How so?" asked Vic, raising an eyebrow.

"We could have crashed."

They drove in silence after that, each watching the rock walls for signs of rockfall. It was an annual problem in most of the Colorado canyons. During the winter months, snow crept into cracks in the granite and froze, fracturing the rock faces. During spring thaw, the rocks broke free and tumbled into the depths of the canyons.

In summer, the monsoons brought the added danger of flooding. Up and down the road in Big Thompson Canyon, signs warned drivers to abandon their vehicles in case of flash floods and climb to safety. Good advice, offered for good reason. In 1976, a Big Thompson Canyon flood had killed one hundred thirty-nine people and injured scores more when a late-afternoon rain shower had dumped eight inches of rain at the headwaters of the Big Thompson River. Unable to absorb the water, the canyon walls funneled the rain into the river, causing the Big Thompson River to overflow its banks and sending a wall of water tumbling toward Loveland. In all, three hundred sixty-one homes, and fifty-two businesses were destroyed in its wake.

Eric glanced up at the sky. Sunshine warmed the canyon rims, and the sun's rays reached down to kiss the canyon floor. There wasn't a cloud in sight.

"You know, for what it's worth, both of those boys came from money backgrounds," said Vic, picking up the thread of conversation where they'd left off. "Their parents doled out the cash, then loosed the boys on the world. Hell, it's no wonder they got into trouble."

"Did they know each other before camp?"

Vic looked surprised and stroked his mustache. "Not that I know of. They were sponsored by different officers. A Cherry Creek officer recommended Tres. He thought it would do the boy good to get out of the city. Douglas County referred Suett. According to the Sheriff's Department, the boy had been keeping his nose clean and just needed a break. Looks like he may get one."

Was he referring to Nora's edict that they recover the truck? wondered Eric. But that didn't make sense. The backpacks inside the vehicle were enough to incriminate the boys.

A few minutes later, they squeezed through "the narrows," a spot where the canyon walls closed in, rising sheer on both sides. Then, the mouth of the canyon opened, spitting them onto the plains.

Fields of blue and side-oats grama, little bluestem, prairie sandreed, and needle-and-thread grasses spread in all directions. Before long, split-rail fences sectioned the land into small acreages. It was a landscape of short prairie grasses; home to the prairie chicken, the mountain plover, long-billed curlew, burrowing owl, lark bunting, and Cassin's sparrow.

To the north, Eric spotted a prairie falcon hunting at the base of a small butte. Above him a gull wheeled in the air. Near the road, a horned lark sunbathed on a wire.

At the junction of U.S. 287, Vic turned left. Ten minutes later, they crossed into Fort Collins, where U.S. 287 became known as College Avenue.

"Okay, start watching for the campus," ordered Vic. "We need to find Pitkin Street."

Eric picked out the campus road just past the visitor center.

Vic turned, and they headed west. "Now keep your eye out for Ellis Hall."

The CSU campus looked like any of a dozen other universities Eric had seen. Nondescript brick buildings plopped down in the middle of wide-open lawns, surrounded by sidewalks teeming with young men and women on foot or on bikes. Music blared. Laughter rang out.

Eric had taken an extension class at CSU once. Founded as an agricultural school in 1870, it was considered to be one of the top "aggie" schools in the country. The signs on the buildings reflected the school's history. They passed the Greenhouse, the Animal Sciences Building, and the Stock Judging Pavilion before a barricade in front of the Anatomy Building blocked the roadway, forcing Vic to turn around.

"Which way now?" Vic muttered after they'd driven back to the first cross street. "Left or right?"

Eric shrugged. "Right." It was a guess, based on the layout of the buildings.

Vic turned south onto East Drive, then west again at Lake Street. He paralleled Pitkin for several blocks, then turned back, ending up at a crossroads again in front of Newsom Hall.

"We're looking for Ellis," said Vic.

"Try over there." Eric pointed to a six-story building a block down on the left. Sure enough, it was Ellis Hall. Constructed of metal and glass, the sprawling dorm sat in the middle of a huge grassy area dotted sparsely with trees and surrounded by parking areas on three sides.

"Okay, Brill said the truck was parked in the resident parking lot along Ellis Drive."

Even squinting into the setting sun, they easily spotted the NPS truck. Painted pale

187

green with a large white circle on the side, it stood out in the sea of black SUVs and small, brightly colored compacts.

Deputy Brill's cruiser was parked kitty-corner across the street from where the NPS truck sat. Vic pulled the Caprice in beside him, rolled down the window on the passenger side, and shut down the car.

"Not much cover," said Vic.

Eric glanced at the wind row of scrawny fir trees. "Any sign of the boys?" he asked.

Deputy Brill shot upright and inclined his head toward the parking lot. "There's your answer now."

Eric followed his nod. A hundred yards away, Justin Suett slunk between a cherry-red Volvo and a white Honda, heading for the NPS truck.

The sun had dropped low on the horizon, and it was hard to see peering into the sun. Eric shaded his eyes and squinted. "Where's the other one?" he asked, his heart pounding.

"Beats me," said Brill.

"Have you seen him today?" asked Vic.

"No, sir. Not even a trace," answered Brill. He took off his hat and wiped a sleeve across his forehead. "Fact is, this is the first sign of life all day."

"Damn," said Vic. "Where is he?"

"He could be inside," suggested Eric. The sun had dropped low on the horizon, its rays bouncing off the windows of Ellis Hall.

"Yeah, with two hundred others," said Brill. "Wait a minute! Suett's not just getting something, he's fired up the truck."

Vic cranked the starter on the cruiser. "Brill, switch your state band to channel eighteen. Suett won't know to monitor. He'd be damn lucky to hear us talk."

"Check," said Brill."

"I'm going to tail the truck. Once we leave the parking lot, head inside and see if you can figure out where our friend was holed up."

"Double check."

Vic put the cruiser in reverse and eased out of the parking space. Stroking his mustache, he kept his eyes on the target. "What do you say we follow Mr. Suett, just to see what he's up to?"

Excitement energized Eric, and he strained forward against the shoulder belt. "For the record, I'll guarantee Nora won't like it."

Vic's eyes narrowed. "But you're game, right?"

"*Ja*, you betcha."

After a cursory check to see if anyone was watching him, Suett backed the truck out of its parking slot. Turning east on Pitkin Street, he headed north on Meridian Avenue, turned back east on Mulberry, then north again on U.S. 287. As the city faded away, Vic dropped back several car lengths.

"You'll find a pair of binoculars in the

glove box. Get them out and keep your eyes on the truck," he ordered.

Eric searched under and around the papers, manuals, and tools crammed into the glove box and eventually turned up a battered leather case. He was surprised to find a good pair of 10 x 50 Zeiss binoculars inside. Pulling them out, he cleaned the lenses, focused on the mountains, adjusted the diopter, then zoomed in on the pickup.

Suett, now clearly in view, reached over and cranked up the tunes. Then, just past Laporte, he turned off at the Bellville exit.

Vic stayed on U.S. 287, and Eric lowered the glasses. "What are you doing?"

"It's an old trick," explained Vic, turning around in the median, and backtracking to the southbound exit. "I don't think Suett spotted us, but if he did, he'll think we drove past."

"*Ja?* The only problem is, now we've lost him."

"He'll turn up. There's only one road out here, and it only goes one direction."

Vic maintained the speed limit, and Eric kept a steady eye out for the NPS truck. The sun dropped from sight as they drove toward the mountains, and twilight settled thick into the valley, rendering the binoculars useless. Where had Suett gone?

Well, there was one consolation, Eric thought. *If they didn't find the truck, he wouldn't be the*

190

only one out of a job.

After the city dropped away, Eric had blinked and nearly missed the town of Laporte, but now the emptiness was complete. Ahead of them the county road stretched away like a black scar on the grassy countryside. Cavernous ditches lined both sides of the road, and the washboard road jostled the car until Eric felt like he'd hitched a ride in a washing machine.

He was beginning to think they should pack it in, when Vic perked up. "Okay, what have we here?"

Eric peered through the windshield. A cluster of darkened buildings flanked the road up ahead. Then, a set of taillights flashed, and the NPS truck slowly pulled off the road.

Chapter 17

Vic slowed the car to a crawl. "Welcome to Bellville, population two. What in God's name is Suett doing out here?"

"Maybe he has some friends in the area," suggested Eric, though by the looks of the place it seemed doubtful.

Vic laughed. "Yeah, except what you see is what you get — downtown Bellville and a few scattered ranch houses. It's been this way since the turn of the century. Though . . ." He thumped the steering wheel. "Come to think of it, Tres's dad is a developer. Could be he's got some interest in the property out here."

"For what possible purpose? Cattle ranching?" Eric looked around and didn't see anything of interest to anyone but a cowman or a birder, and there wasn't much money in bird sanctuaries.

Vic pointed toward the mountains. "The Poudre River runs down through there, then just over a ways is Lory State Park and the Horsetooth Reservoir. People have been talking about building up this area with condominiums and tract housing developments for years. There are already a couple of big dude ranches in the area."

They had drawn close enough now for Eric to distinguish the two buildings that made up the town — an old carriage house on the left and a wooden farmhouse that faced it from across the street.

It was obvious that the carriage house served as the town's post office. Constructed of brick and mortar, the huge wooden doors, built to accommodate buggies, were painted bright red. A small metal door had been cut into the bricks, over which the postmaster had hung a green sign reading "Bellville," and a light with a low-watt bulb.

The farmhouse had been converted into a general store. From the looks of it, the building had been added on to a couple of times. The roof lines varied — some were peaked, some were flat. The siding, though painted the same shade of yellow, had been cut from different styles of board.

Lights shone in the distant windows of the scattered ranch houses, but there were no homes built near town. A short way down the road was a one-pump gas station, boarded up tight.

Somewhere in the distance, a dog bayed. Vic killed the headlights and coasted the car to a stop in the alley next to the Post Office. "There's Tres," he whispered. "See him?"

The young man stood in the darkened window of the General Store. Tall and gangly, his blond hair jutted out at odd angles, highlighted by the glow of the low-watt bulb above the Post Office sign. He pressed his nose to the glass and peered out. Was he watching for Suett?

Eric knew the sheriff's car was invisible in the shadows, but he drew back in his seat anyway. He feared the boy could sense them, and the thought raised the hair on the back of his neck.

Then, out of nowhere, Suett appeared, crabbing his way up the sidewalk with some sort of bundle in his arms.

"Can you see what he's carrying?" Eric asked. He raised the binoculars, but the dim light wouldn't filter through the prisms. Suett glanced around, then, with the coast clear, scurried across the road to the General Store.

Tres opened the door. "About time, a-hole."

"Shut your face, dude," replied Suett.

Tres held the door, letting Suett sidle in. The boy turned sideways. He shimmied through the cracked doorway, light from the street catching on the bundle in his arms.

Eric craned forward in his seat. "He's carrying an armload of fusees! Do you see that?"

"Damn," said Vic. "That's not good." Reaching up, he switched the overhead light switch to the off position, then eased open his door. Eric reached for his own door handle.

"Where are you going?" he asked. "Do you have a plan?"

"Sure," replied Vic. "I want you to get on the radio to Brill and tell him to send backup. Then, you stay put and keep your eye out for the cavalry, while I go over there and see if I can prevent those boys from burning down the General Store."

A flash of annoyance caused Eric to frown. He didn't like being assigned to dispatch duty. "Those boys" were in possession of an NPS vehicle and may have bashed Wayne over the head before stealing his truck. "I think I should come with you," he said.

"No, you are going to call Brill, then wait for him like I told you to," ordered Vic, squeezing out from under the wheel. "I'll be back in a flash."

Eric watched the older man scoot around the back side of the Post Office, then he glanced at his watch. Adjusting the radio, he keyed the mike. "Deputy Brill, come in, over."

When the deputy answered, Eric told him how they had followed the truck and found the boys. "Send backup. Over."

"Ten-four, I'm on the way. ETA in under thirty. Out."

Eric reclipped the handset to the radio then glanced back at his watch. It had taken less than two minutes to contact Brill, and, in the meantime, Vic had disappeared.

Inside the General Store, the boys had lit several candles. The same light that made it easy for the boys to see, made it easy for Eric to watch them while they looted the store's camping supplies. Trip after trip to the shelves, they busied themselves with dumping bundles of ready-made firewood and presswood logs into a pile in the center aisle. They were making a bonfire.

The realization caused another shiver of fear to ripple down Eric's back. Where the heck was Vic?

Suddenly, Suett stooped and picked up a fusee. Two fusees.

"No, man. Don't be a fool," Eric whispered, his knee jiggling with nervous energy.

Suett marched around the pyre, twirling the fusees like they were a majorette's batons. He tossed them higher and higher, caught them, spun them, then tossed them aloft, again and again.

Unable to sit and wait for catastrophe, Eric decided to follow Vic and eased open his door. Even if Vic managed to get into the store through the back, the boys could bolt out the front. Eric figured if he positioned himself well, he could stop them from getting away.

He studied the buildings. To get across the street without being seen, he'd have to stay in the shadows. To do that, he needed to cut across on the west of the General Store, avoiding the path cut by the overhead light.

Climbing out of the car, Eric made a dash toward the rear of the Post Office. Gravel crunched beneath his heels. He winced at the noise. Had they heard him? Reaching the building, he pressed his back to the bricks, and listened. Had he heard other footsteps?

After waiting a moment or two, he decided what he'd heard were his own footsteps, and he inched himself forward along the rough surface of the bricks. After another moment, he threw caution aside and sprinted to the back of the building.

A wide parking lot had been carved out of the hillside. Graveled, with high embankments, it opened in a sweeping half-circle away from the building. Midpoint, Suett had parked the NPS truck in the postmaster's reserved slot.

Walking over to the truck, Eric peered into the cab. The boys' backpacks still littered the passenger side floor. Candy wrappers comingled with Coke cans on the seat, and a set of keys dangled from the ignition.

Yanking open the truck door, Eric jerked the keys from the ignition, then moved to the rear of the truck. A box of fusees sat in the truck bed, and he hauled the box to the end of the tailgate, rummaging through it and counting the fusees. The brand the NPS used came in boxes of twenty-four. Counting by twos, he came up with twelve left.

He rechecked the numbers, then added them to the two that had been in Wayne's pack and the one that had been in Wayne's hand, coming up with fifteen. Which meant Suett and Tres had used — or were about to use — nine.

"Put your hands up," ordered a deep voice.

Eric turned to see who had issued the command and found himself staring down the double barrel of a shotgun.

"I said, put your hands up. In the air. Where I can see 'em." A young cowboy in a white hat, white shirt, boots, and jeans, and wearing a belt buckle the size of a small piece of toast, shouldered the gun.

"I'm a ranger," said Eric, complying with the order. "I'm with the National Park Service." Had the boys staked a lookout? What if this was one of their friends?

"I don't care if you're with the FBI," said the cowboy. "What are you doin' here?" He stood, one hip cocked, holding the gun steady.

"Two juveniles stole this truck. The sheriff and I followed them here." Eric started to drop his hands, but the cowboy gestured for him to keep them up. Eric jerked his head toward the buildings. "They're about to burn down your General Store."

The cowboy's eyes darted in the direction of the street. His view of the General Store was obscured by the Post Office building. "I don't see nothin'," he said.

"If you don't believe me, check for yourself." Eric wished he could see the cowboy's expression, but his hat obscured his face. "Plus, I have an ID in my pocket that proves who I am."

Not to mention, I'm wearing a uniform.

"Stay put," the cowboy ordered. He lowered his gun and stepped away, and Eric dropped his hands. A low growl stopped him in mid-motion. A German shepherd sat a few feet away, his ears laid back, his nose wrinkled.

"Good dog, Bingo," said the cowboy without turning around. "Guard."

"Good dog," repeated Eric, raising his hands back into the air.

Bingo relaxed.

The cowboy edged his way along the back of the Post Office, peeked his head around the corner, and whistled softly.

Bingo's ears pricked forward.

"See," said Eric, pointing with his right hand.

Bingo barred his teeth, and crouched.

"It's okay, boy," said the cowboy, turning back. "It looks like this fella's tellin' us the truth." He shouldered the gun, and Bingo sauntered in for a pat on the head. "Did you say the sheriff's with your —"

"*Ja.*"

"Where is he?"

Eric shrugged. "I don't know. He got out of the car about ten minutes ago. I haven't seen him since. I figure he's in back of the General Store, since there aren't many other ways to get inside without being spotted."

The cowboy jerked his head toward the street. "If it's all the same to you, I'm thinkin' of goin' in the front door with my dog and shotgun. One way or another, we oughta be able to nail these clowns."

Eric agreed. "That was sort of my plan, too." *Short of walking in with a dog and a gun.*

The cowboy raised his eyebrows.

"How about this?" said Eric. "You stand guard here and make sure neither one of the boys leaves through the front. I'll cross the street and go around back of the General Store and see if I can find the sheriff. He may have a different plan for us. Either way, I'll come back and signal you if we want you to come in through the front."

The cowboy tipped back his hat, and a thick mane of brown hair fell across his forehead. "Sure, I guess we can try it that way. Just so's you know, though." The cowboy gestured toward his dog. "We ain't fixin' to let them burn down the General Store. Bingo here is sorta partial to their bones."

"I understand," said Eric. "Just give me a couple of minutes."

Figuring a couple was all he would get, Eric waited until he was sure it was clear and hurried across the street. Turning away from the main entrance, he kept to the shadows and the sidewalk along the front corner of the building. When Eric reached the side of the General Store, the sidewalk ended and the ditch picked up. Deep, and three feet across, the ditch was too wide for Eric to negotiate from a standing jump, so he took a run at it. His feet landed on the edge, sending a shower of scree clattering into the ditch. Clambering for a foothold, his feet churned the earth at the lip of the ditch. He surged forward, gained solid ground, and froze. Had Tres or Suett heard him?

Pressing himself against the side of the building, he counted to ten.

When the cowboy waved, Eric pushed away from the rough bricks and scrambled over the uneven ground toward the back of the store. Rounding the corner, he stumbled over the sheriff, who was sitting on the ground.

"Vic!"

"Sshhhh!"

Eric dropped to one knee and whispered, "What are you doin'? What happened?"

"I put my foot through an old root cellar door, or a well cover. I couldn't yell for fear of alerting our friends inside." Vic jerked his head back toward the road. "Why aren't you waiting for Brill?"

Eric ignored the question, patting the ground around Vic's leg. The sheriff's boot was jammed through a two-by-six-inch board. Eric tried pulling Vic's foot free.

Vic groaned. "That's ripping my ankle to shreds."

Eric probed the opening with his fingers. Shards of wood jutted out at odd angles. Dirt was caked on top of the boards, cementing them in place. An upward pull caused the boards to knit together. Eric tried pushing them down. What he needed was a shovel.

"Stop, Eric. If we make any more noise, they're bound to hear us."

Eric sat back on his heels. "*Vell*, you can't stay here. They're getting ready to torch the building."

The sheriff stroked his mustache, then wet his lips, "Did you get ahold of Brill?"

"*Ja*, he's on his way."

"Good. Do you know how to use a gun?"

"*Ja*." Though he didn't care much for guns, Eric knew how to shoot. "Besides, we have help." Eric told him about the cowboy and the dog.

"Do you think he's trustworthy?" asked Vic.

"He didn't shoot me."

Vic contemplated Eric's answer, then shrugged. "That's good enough for me." Unclipping his handcuffs from his belt, he handed them to Eric along with the gun. "Go signal the cowboy that you're going inside. Give yourself two minutes. Then, slip in through the back and yell 'freeze.' Real loud, and real mean. That should be enough to stop those boys in their tracks. Then, after you cuff them together, come back and get me out of here."

Sweat beaded on Eric's forehead. The plan was simple, but Vic hadn't seen the way Suett had been dancing around the bonfire. Or how bent Tres had been on building a flammable mountain. Throw the cowboy and his dog into the mix, and it was hard to tell what might happen.

Eric backtracked around the building. At the edge of the ditch, he raised his free arm above his head. The cowboy mimicked his action. Eric held up two fingers, then pointed with the gun barrel toward his watch. The cowboy tipped his hat and pushed himself upright off the corner of the Post Office.

Turning back, Eric prayed the cowboy had understood. Skirting Vic, he headed for the back stairs.

Three steps climbed to the back door, and Eric eased his weight onto the first step. A screech sliced through the night.

"Keep to the outside," whispered Vic. "The *out*side."

His advice made sense, decided Eric. The edges were joist. There would be less weight displacement on the boards there than in the middle. He tried again. This time the step only groaned. *Better.*

Once on the platform, Eric tried turning the handle on the back door. The handle wouldn't budge. "It's locked," he whispered. "What do I do now?"

"What kind of lock is it?" asked Vic. "Some you can pick with a toothpick, some with a credit card. If worse comes to worse, you wait another minute to ensure your cowboy's in position out front, then you shoot it open."

Rambo tactics, thought Eric. He hadn't bargained for this.

What amazed him more was the fine line between cop and criminal. Too bad he'd never learned to pick a lock. He might have made a good police officer.

Eric tested the door with his shoulder. There was some give to the wood, and he figured he could break the door down if he hit it right. Not without making some noise, but still better than a gunshot.

He counted to thirty. "Here goes."

Eric's shoulder hit. The door banged inward, slamming against a fire extinguisher that was hanging on the back wall. Regaining his feet, he discovered himself in an entryway facing another door. He jiggled the handle. *Damn it!* Didn't anyone trust anyone anymore?

He butted his shoulder against the wood, but this time there was no give. A wrenching pain cut through his collarbone. *Just great.* Standing back, he shot a bullet in the lock and kicked open the door.

"Hey, what the —" Suett stood in the center of the room. He held the fusees coupled into a two-foot chain. Tres stared, slack-jawed, and dribbled the remnants of a can of lighter fluid onto his foot.

"Put the fusees down," ordered Eric.

Suett held up a butane lighter. "Stay away from me."

"I said, put the fusees down," repeated Eric, giving his best Arnold Schwarzenegger imitation.

Suett listened about as well as any bad guy Arnold ever had to face.

"Back off, or I'll light it," he threatened. Flicking the butane lighter, Suett poised the flame under the wick of the fusee.

Tres's eyes grew big. "Hey, man, what are you doing? You can't light that with us in here."

"Shut your face, dude."

Eric saw the wick spark, and sucked in a sharp breath. "You don't want to do that, Suett." *Where the hell was the cowboy?*

"How do you know my name?"

Eric heard a loud bang, then the front window shattered. Tres bolted for the door.

"Don't shoot!" yelled Eric.

There was another explosion. This time buckshot splintered the floor near Suett's feet.

"That's it, dude." Suett lit the fusees. The wick curled, then flamed, and the fusees burst to life. Like a giant sparkler, embers showered from it to the floor.

Bingo barked and jumped through the window, knocking Suett to the floor. The fusees flew from his hand, tumbling in slow motion, spinning in the air like a giant pinwheel. Eric reached to catch them, and missed.

The fusees bounced once, then nosedived into the pyre.

The room ignited in a gigantic explosion of flame.

Chapter 18

Fire erupted in leaping flames and boiled toward the ceiling. Heat pulsed in waves along the wooden floor. Eric shied away. Glancing up, he saw the cowboy framed in the doorway.

"Bingo. Here, boy." The man whistled.

Eric shielded his face against the wall of flames. Smoke burned his eyes, making them tear. The world swam.

Bingo yelped, then raced for the door and his master, his fur smoldering.

Where was Tres? Eric searched for the boy. He hadn't seen him since he'd bolted. With luck the kid had escaped through the front door and been collared by the cowboy.

Suett lay on the floor near Eric's feet. Orange tongues of flame lapped in circles around his body. Eric needed to do something quickly, or the boy would burn to death. Bending down, he tried rousting him. "Suett!"

When he didn't respond, Eric tried pulling the boy to his feet. The kid's dead weight, combined with his size, made moving him alone nearly impossible.

Eric cast about for alternatives. Behind

him, the flames leaped around the base of the old store's shelves. Tin cans exploded, their contents swollen by heat. Microwave popcorn burst in its bag. He tried not to think about what would happen when the flames reached the ammunition most of these old country stores carried.

There had to be something . . . The fire extinguisher! There had been one on the wall when he'd crashed through the door.

Eric jammed his gun behind him in the waistband of his pants. He'd seen it done on TV. With luck, he wouldn't blow a hole in his ass.

Racing to the back room, he ripped the fire extinguisher off the wall and pulled the pin. Juggling the heavy red canister, he squeezed the trigger, spewing foam onto the fire, driving it back toward the center of the room. The fire dodged the artificial snow. Forced to find other routes, the flames lapped along the baseboards and circled in behind.

Suett groaned.

"Hey, can you hear me?" yelled Eric.

The kid groaned again. "My head. I think I busted my head open."

Eric jostled the boy with his foot. "Get up."

Suett rolled onto his side and stopped moving.

"Listen to me. You have to get up." Eric

prodded the boy again, spraying foam around his inert form. The fire growled, and a fountain of sparks flew toward the ceiling. An ember landed, skittering along the splintered wood. Dry timbers crackled and flamed.

Realizing the only way he was going to get the kid out of there was to drag him, Eric doused the floor. Then, pitching the fire extinguisher aside, he reached for Suett's arm.

"Let me help," said Tres, materializing from out of the fire and grabbing his friend's other arm. Eric stared for a moment, then together they pulled Suett out of the flames.

The back door stood open, and the two of them dragged Suett outside and down the stairs, moving him deep into the meadow away from the General Store. Flames followed, licking the doorway and snaking into the grass before doubling back toward the building.

By the time Eric figured they'd moved Suett a safe distance from the burning building, the cowboy and Bingo had circled around back.

"Check on the sheriff!" Eric shouted, dropping Suett's arm, and racing back toward the General Store. The building glowed a deep orange at its edges.

The cowboy reached Vic first. Laying his shotgun on the ground, he bent down and examined the situation. "We're going to need a winch to get him outta here."

Sirens blared in the distance, either Deputy Brill with the cavalry or the fire department. But either way, there wasn't time to wait. Orange and blue flames spiraled through the dark night, dancing along the building's eaves. The timbers dripped splinters of wood like molten lava. The General Store stood poised to collapse.

The cowboy glanced at Eric. "There ain't no way we're going to kick it apart. There's too much dirt and grass keeping the boards solid."

Eric eyed the shotgun. "Can we weaken the boards by shooting them?"

Even in the dark, Vic paled. "Hold on a minute. That's my leg you're talking about."

Eric didn't speak. He pointed to the building, the flames licking through cracks in the walls, the fire destined to break free any minute. "We can't wait."

Vic glanced between the gun and the building. "What do you have in that thing? Slugs?"

"Birdshot."

Eric frowned. Small gauge pellets that scattered.

"Can you shoot away from my foot?" asked Vic. "I mean, we only need to weaken the boards enough to break them. I don't want my foot blown off."

"I'm a pretty good shot," assured the cowboy, drawing a bead over Vic's shoulder.

"Cover your ears."

"Hang on," said Eric. "We need to find something to cover his body." All Eric had was the fleece vest in the car. "Does anyone have a coat?"

"I might have something in the back of the patrol car," said Vic.

"I've got a saddle blanket in my truck," said the cowboy.

Eric perked up. "That would work. Where is it?"

"I parked it by the gas station."

"Is it unlocked?" asked Tres, leaving Suett to join them. "I can get it."

The cowboy hesitated, then pitched the boy the keys. "Go with him, Bingo."

Tres made a dash for the gas station, and Bingo set off after him.

Eric wondered if the boy would come back. This was a prime opportunity for him to make a break. But, he'd chosen to help save his friend. Now he had the opportunity to show his real colors.

"Don't worry none," said the cowboy. "Bingo'll bring him back."

The fire flared. Boards popped and crackled. Sirens wailed in the distance, and Eric thought he saw flashes of blue and white through a wind row of trees that cut the field. "Hang in there, Vic. *Når nøden er størst, er hjelpen nærmest.*"

"Excuse me?"

211

"It's an old Norse saying. *When the need is at its greatest, help is at its closest.*"

"Yeah? Well my money's on the kid."

The seconds ticked by. Suett groaned, but didn't try to rise. The cowboy drew a bead on the boards near Vic's feet. Vic cupped his ears, leaning away.

When the roof erupted in flames, the cowboy's finger squeezed pressure on the trigger.

"Wait!" shouted Eric, pointing. Tres bolted toward them across the field with Bingo bouncing at his heels.

"I got it, man. And look what else I found," Tres shouted, bench-pressing an axe above his head.

"Here. Give it to me," said the cowboy.

Tres handed the axe to the cowboy and pitched the horse blanket to Vic.

"I hope you're good with an axe?" said Vic.

"I only chopped my own leg once," promised the cowboy. He winked, then swung. Vic winced.

On the third chop, the board splintered. Above them, the roof snapped and caved in, throwing up a shower of sparks.

"Let's go, let's go!" shouted Vic. He tried standing, but his foot buckled under him. "The damn thing's gone to sleep."

The cowboy pitched the axe. He and Eric each looped one of Vic's arms across their shoulders. Tres led the way.

"Go, go, go!" shouted the cowboy. The men dragged Vic into the meadow. Behind them the building groaned and timbers snapped. The fire crackled, leaping high into the air and showering a cascade of sparks down on their heads.

Reaching Suett, the four of them collapsed to the ground. Eric glanced back. The General Store looked like a giant bonfire. Blue and white lights flashed at the corner. Bingo ran in circles, and barked.

An hour later, leaning against the fender of Vic's Caprice, Eric watched the firemen hose down the embers that were once Bellville's General Store. The fire department had arrived on Deputy Brill's heels, with a 600-gallon pumper truck and a five-man crew. A rancher had spotted the flames and called in the alarm.

"I'd say we're almost done here," said Vic, limping across the parking lot toward Eric. "Are you about ready?"

Eric nodded, then glanced over at the NPS truck still parked in the postmaster's slot. "Nora isn't going to be happy you impounded the truck."

"I'll handle Nora."

Eric grinned. *Nobody handled Nora,* he thought.

"Besides," Vic continued, "I have to impound it to preserve the evidence."

"So what's going to happen to the boys?" Eric asked, staring at Tres in the backseat of Brill's cruiser. The boy's head was bent, his blond hair blackened from soot and smoke. Suett had been air-lifted to a hospital in Fort Collins an hour ago.

"Suett will probably be in the hospital awhile. Weeks, maybe. He suffered some nasty burns." Vic jerked his thumb at Tres. "He goes to juvi."

"That boy helped save Suett's life," said Eric, hoping somehow restating the facts would help. "Yours too."

"Look, son, don't kid yourself. Tres Kennedy is accountable for what happened here tonight." Vic hesitated. "Though I'd be surprised if he lights any more fires."

"*Ja*, why's that?"

Vic tipped his head. "It's another old saying. 'A burnt child shuns the fire.'"

Eric gazed out at the glowing embers, dying like the coals of a stirred campfire. "*Brent barn skyr ilden.*" He glanced at Vic. "We can only hope."

Deputy Brill shouted, and Eric turned. The officer hurried across the street, with the cowboy and Bingo in tow.

"Look what the cowboy pulled out of the fire." Brill dumped an armload of fusees on to the hood of Vic's car. "More evidence."

The cowboy jammed his hands in his pockets. "It wasn't nothing. I saw 'em sittin' by the door. I nearly forgot I had 'em until Deputy Brill, here, started asking questions."

"I count eight," said Brill.

Eric pushed off the fender. "That can't be right."

"Why not?" asked the cowboy. Bingo growled.

"Because Suett had two in his hands." Eric bent down and counted the fusees himself. *Eight.* "It doesn't add up. Eight plus two makes ten."

"Are you going somewhere with this?" asked Vic.

"*Ja,* the ten the boys had plus the twelve in the truck, plus the two in Wayne's pack equals twenty-four."

"Maybe he breathed in too much smoke," remarked the cowboy.

"No," said Eric. "When you add them together, you've accounted for a full box of fusees."

Vic frowned. The cowboy and Bingo looked puzzled, tilting their heads at a similar angle.

"So what?" demanded Brill. "So they're all accounted for. I don't see the problem."

"So where did the fusee in Wayne's hand come from?" asked Eric. "Don't you get it? The National Park Service is holding Wayne responsible for lighting Eagle Cliff Fire with a fusee he would never have had."

"Oh, come on, Linenger," scoffed Brill.

"You know, I liked Devlin, but so what if he had another fusee? Maybe he carried an extra one in his pack."

"Not Wayne," insisted Eric. "Vic, you know how meticulous he was about things. 'Everything in its place, and a place for everything.' "

Vic stroked his mustache. "That's true. He was orderly."

Eric picked up a fusee. "It's fact. Wayne came off every fire and repacked according to a checklist. Two fusees went in the pack, and twenty-two fusees in the box. Extras were placed on the fire trucks, or stockpiled for replenishing boxes. I'm telling you, the man wouldn't have deviated. It's how he'd done it for eighteen years. It's how he accounted for supplies."

Vic put his hand on Eric's shoulder. "Be honest, son. You know as well as anyone, Wayne hadn't been acting like himself."

"I'll give you that," Eric conceded. "He seemed different the past year and a half, but he always came through. I'm telling you, he would never have deviated from procedure."

"Can you prove it?" asked Vic.

Eric toyed with the fusee. "No."

Brill snorted. "Of course not."

The cowboy and Bingo shifted positions and sidled away, extricating themselves from the conversation.

"I thought, in this country, someone was

innocent until proven guilty *beyond* the shadow of a doubt," said Eric, ignoring their departure. "I'm beginning to wonder."

"The term is 'reasonable doubt,'" said Vic, "and based on the evidence . . ." He looked down at his boots. "Look, I drew the same conclusion as the fire investigation team. The same conclusion as a lot of people. Like it or not, the evidence all points to Wayne."

Eric picked up another fusee and linked the two together in a chain. "What would it take to convince you that you're wrong?"

Vic raised his eyebrows. "Proof. *Real* proof. Some good solid evidence that convinces me the investigation team findings were wrong."

Eric thought of Linda Verbiscar's tape. "What about a video that shows someone else lighting the fire?"

"Film, tapes, photographs — they can all be altered," said Brill. "They're not admissible in court."

"True," admitted Vic. "Though, it might make me rethink my position. Still, without something else, you're back in the same boat."

That left the fusees, thought Eric. Maybe the investigators had overlooked some physical evidence at the crime scene. "If I can bring you proof, will you reopen the case?"

"No," said Brill.

Vic shook his head. "It's out of my jurisdiction. That section of the park falls in

217

Larimer County, and they deferred to the Park Service investigators."

"I thought you sat in on the hearings."

"I did. So did Bernie Crandall. That doesn't mean either one of us has any clout."

"Are you telling me that there's nothing you can do?"

"I'm afraid that's the bottom line, son. This one's out of my hands."

Chapter 19

It was after midnight by the time Vic dropped Eric off at the cabin, and Eric was hours overdue for his meeting with Linda Verbiscar. Driving up the hill past the Inn on 34, he'd checked to see if there were any lights on at the inn. The buildings had all been dark. Now, unlocking his own door, he wondered what to do next.

The message light was blinking. It was from Linda Verbiscar. She wanted to meet at her place, in the morning, *before* she left for work. "Say around 4 a.m."

That gave him less than four hours.

Stripping off his soiled uniform, he stepped into the shower. The hot water felt good pounding against his skin, washing away not only the grime of the fire but the anger he felt about what had happened to Wayne. A senseless death that looked more and more like murder.

Yet, for the first time since he'd found his friend's body, Eric felt hope. Hope that he could find some evidence to prove the investigation team wrong. Evidence that would save Jackie's home and give Tamara back her dreams of a college education.

Eric twisted, letting the spray pummel the knots from his back and the ache from his shoulder. He basked in the steam, mulling over the events of the day.

If Tres Kennedy's account of what had happened was true, Eric's suspect list had dwindled by two. According to Tres, he and Justin Suett had never seen Wayne Devlin. They'd stuck to the trees closest to the road. It was the easiest path to freedom.

They'd stumbled upon Wayne's truck, in the trees on the Youth Camp side of Prospect Point. The keys were in the ignition, and they'd taken the opportunity when it knocked.

A radio news flash about their disappearance was what steered them north away from Denver. Knowing they couldn't go home, they'd headed to Bellville. Tres's father was part owner of the General Store. Tres knew how to get in, and Suett's brother had a friend at CSU they could hit up for money. The General Store fire had been spontaneous. A spur-of-the-moment thing that had flared out of control.

Eric shut off the shower and reached for a towel. Their story made sense. If Tres and Suett had come across Wayne, bashed him in the head, and wanted to camouflage the crime scene, they would have used one of Wayne's fusees to light the fire. Based on the number of fusees that had been accounted

for, Eric knew that whoever killed Wayne —
and he was more convinced than ever
Wayne's death had not been an accident —
had brought a fusee of their own.

Eric lay down on the bed. The next thing
he knew, he was being jostled awake by the
alarm clock. He stretched, wincing at the
pain in his shoulder, then pulled on a pair of
jeans, a turtleneck, and tennis shoes. A shave,
clean teeth, and a mug of coffee later, he
headed out into the predawn morning to
scrape his windows.

He made good time. There were no other
cars on the road. Downtown Elk Park was
deserted, except for the bakery crew who
bustled behind the shop windows on Main
Street. All the other stores were shuttered
against the night.

Turning onto U.S. 34, Eric started watching for the inn. The streetlamp on the highway was out, and he nearly missed the turn.
Cranking the wheel hard, he jounced into the
parking lot, spewing gravel against the metal
lamppost.

The inn was designed in a horseshoe configuration around the swimming pool. The
hotel office sat in front, like a plug gently
freed from its drain. Cabins ringed the en-
clave, scattered in random groupings on the
outside fringes of a graveled, circular
driveway.

Cabin G was perched on top of the hill be-

221

hind the hotel, a good twenty feet back from the drive. The structure — billed as a one-bedroom, one-bath unit, with a kitchen–living room–dining room combination — boasted all of six-hundred square feet. The outer shell — constructed of sawed-off logs and mustard-colored plaster — sagged precariously on a cinder block foundation. No lights illuminated any of the windows, and the front drapes were drawn tight.

Had Verbiscar overslept their meeting?

Parking his car next to her Honda, Eric climbed out of the truck and jogged up the path to the cabin. Ice crystals coated the pathway, and the grass crackled beneath his shoes. In the meadow, a coyote yipped. An early bird twittered. He listened, hoping to hear it again. Then, the hotel generator kicked on and drowned out all other sound.

Eric reached the cabin door and hesitated. Did he really want to wake her if she was asleep? Then again, if she had to be at work, he would be doing her a favor.

He tapped. "Verbiscar?"

No answer.

He tapped louder and raised his voice. "Verbiscar."

Still no answer.

Cameraman Charlie's vehicle was parked in front of the motel, so she hadn't left with him. Where the heck was she?

Convinced there were no signs of life at

the cabin, Eric headed for the media van. A red, white, and blue banner painted on the side proclaimed it the property of "KEPC-TV, Your News Channel." The van was locked up tight, but Eric peered through the windows. Mounds of camera equipment were piled behind the driver's seat, and a parking tag in the window read "129."

Room 129 was located on the outside of the horseshoe, directly across from the van. In contrast to the darkened cabin, a dim bedside light backlit the room. Eric could clearly see two people inside.

Maybe Verbiscar and Charlie had more in common than the morning news?

The couple lay entwined on the bed. Definitely pleasure, not business then. Eric debated coming back later, or waiting. They'd have to come out at some point.

Then, remembering the interview request and the threats regarding the tape, Eric rapped hard on the door.

The couple stirred.

Eric rapped again. Through the filmy gauze of the window curtain, he saw someone climb out of bed. Charlie answered the door. "Yeah?"

Minus his baseball cap, the cameraman's short dark hair stuck out in unruly spikes. Minus the camera, he looked small. And naked. He'd dragged the comforter with him and stood clutching it at his waist.

"What do you want?" he demanded.

"Is Verbiscar here?" asked Eric.

"Are you nuts?" Charlie rubbed his eyes. "Why would she be here? What time is it?"

Eric glanced at his watch. "A little after the hour. She was supposed to meet me here at four."

"Did you try her cabin?"

Eric ignored the cameraman's "you're such an idiot" tone and nodded. "I just came from there."

"Well, I haven't seen her, buddy. Sorry." Charlie started to shut the door, but Eric pushed it back.

"I really need to find her."

Charlie scowled. "Then maybe you should try the studio? She goes on at six today."

KEPC-TV didn't have studio space in town.

"The van's empty," said Eric. "Besides, she said to meet her here."

The woman in bed shifted. "Who is it, Charlie?"

Eric's mouth went dry at the sound of the voice. He recognized the girlish tone, the pouty whine. Charlie the cameraman was sleeping with Tamara Devlin.

"Just some —"

Eric coughed, and slashing a finger across his throat, gave Charlie the universal sign for "cut." The cameraman looked stunned.

"Thanks," mouthed Eric. "You've been a big help."

"Who?" repeated Tamara.

"Nobody," said Charlie, recovering quickly. "Just a wrong room."

"At four in the morning?"

The door cut off the rest of their conversation, and Eric headed back to his truck.

Tamara Devlin. He wondered if Jackie knew where her daughter was. Probably not. A guy like Charlie didn't fit into Jackie's plans. Tamara was smart enough to know it. No doubt she kept Charlie under wraps.

Eric considered going back and dragging her out of the hotel room. But, she was eighteen, old enough to do what she wanted. It was a good thing Wayne was dead. Her promiscuity would have killed him.

Climbing the hill, Eric could see the Honda still parked in the pullout. Moonlight brightened the sky, and highlighted contours in the land. To the west, mountains stretched along the horizon, a jagged spine of dark granite against the moonlit sky. The white frost on the grass blades glowed with a neon tinge.

Eric stared down at the grass. *That's odd,* he thought. There were shapes and tracks imprinted on the ground, patterns etched into the frost.

Squatting near the path, he reached out a hand and touched a footprint. The heat from his fingers melted the edge of the image, but it was clear the print belonged to him. Not many people wore size thirteen shoes. But there were other prints, too. A smaller set of footprints, along with a set of tire tracks similar to the ones he had noticed up on Eagle Cliff Mountain the day he'd discovered Wayne Devlin's body.

A sudden, sickening thought propelled him toward the cabin. What if the person Linda Verbiscar planned to expose had learned about the tape?

Hadn't she told Eric she'd talked to someone else? What if she'd said something to the wrong person?

One thing he knew for sure, someone else had been there earlier this morning. Eric banged on the cabin door. "Verbiscar? Are you in there?" He tried the handle. The door was locked. "Verbiscar?"

He pressed his ear close to the door and listened. Had he heard someone moan?

Lights blinked on at the hotel. Somewhere a door opened, and a man yelled. "Hey, shut up out there. People are trying to sleep."

Eric banged again. "Verbiscar, I know you're in there."

He moved around to the side of the building and tried peering in a window. Dark thick drapes covered the glass.

"Hey, pervert," shouted the hotel guest. "Get away from there."

Eric responded by ordering the guy to call

the manager. "I think the lady who rents this cabin needs help."

"Seriously?" hollered the guest, reaching for what turned out to be a warm pair of sweatpants.

"Seriously."

Lights flashed on in more of the hotel rooms. Eric moved around to the next window. This curtain was only partially closed, but he still couldn't see anything. Only several large, dark shapes. The outlines of furniture, maybe?

Eric circled the cabin. He checked every window, knocking and calling out Verbiscar's name, to no avail. *Wait.*

Had he heard something? A whine, maybe?

He pressed his ear against the cabin wall.

"Errri." The sound jarred him to the bone, burrowing into the marrow like the screech of a wounded animal.

"Shit, what was that?"

Eric jumped at the sound of the man's voice behind him. Judging by his attire, he was the Good Samaritan guest.

Dressed in baggy sweatpants, tennis shoes, and a North Face jacket, the man tugged at the zipper to cover his exposed chest. "Do you think that was a cat?" he asked, a hopeful note to his voice.

Eric leaned back toward the wall. "Verbiscar, is that you?"

No response.

"I don't hear anything," whispered the man, hunkering down beside Eric. "It had to be a cat."

Eric put a finger to his lips.

"Errriiiiii."

Both men jumped.

"Eerie is right," said the hotel guest.

"Hold on, Verbiscar!" yelled Eric. "We're getting help."

The hotel guest hit the circular drive at a dead run. His feet hammered the dirt, pounding a drumbeat in his haste to reach the hotel office. Eric followed, allowing the steep pitch of the hill to propel his body ahead of his feet. At the driveway, he swerved toward the truck.

"I'll use the radio to call dispatch," he yelled. "You see if the manager has a key."

The man shot him a thumbs-up.

Eric reached for the radio and keyed the mike. "Dispatch, come in, over."

"Dispatch. Over."

"I have an emergency at the Inn on 34. Possible injuries."

"Ten-four. Please identify yourself."

Eric gave her his name, directions to the Inn on 34, then signed off. He had just shut the door of his truck, when the hotel guest returned from the office with a gray-haired man in tow.

"He's the manager," explained the guest.

The older man, dressed in flannel pajamas,

228

a terry cloth robe, and wool slippers, kept rubbing his eyes. "What is this all about?"

Eric explained. It took several minutes to convince him, but finally the manager patted down the pockets of his robe and produced a set of keys.

"This better be good, young man."

"Please hurry."

The manager knocked on the door. "Ms. Verbiscar?" When no sound came from inside, he shook his head. "I don't hear anything."

"Well we did, didn't we?" said the hotel guest, closing ranks with Eric. "I'll bet you money somebody's hurt in there."

The manager waffled. "I don't know. This little escapade has lawsuit written all over it. Barging in on guests at this time of the morning . . . I mean, you don't know what we might be interrupting. Maybe we should wait for the police to get here, and have you tell them —"

"Waiting is not an option," said Eric, snatching the keys out of the older man's hand.

"Hey, give me those back!"

"I'm a forest ranger," said Eric, forcing the key into the lock. "I'll take full responsibility."

"You have no authority," protested the manager. "Be assured, this is going to rest on your —"

"Head. I know." Eric turned the key and cautiously opened the door. Inside, the drapes were pulled down. The room lay in a puddle of darkness.

Reaching up, Eric flipped on the light. Blood covered everything — the walls, the furniture, the floor. The refrigerator looked like a kindergartner had finger painted a picture on it in red.

Eric gagged, covering his mouth and nose.

"What the hell happened in here?" cried the hotel guest.

"I don't know." Eric scanned the room. From the blood on the floor, it looked like Verbiscar had dragged herself into the bedroom.

"Anybody here?" hollered Eric. The wood floors bounced his words off the ceilings and walls. His voice echoed back with a tinny ring. "Hello?"

"Maybe she drove herself to the hospital?" asked the guest. He looked white beneath his tan. The hotel manager had gone back outside and busied himself keeping curious hotel patrons at bay.

"Stay here," ordered Eric. "Keep an eye out for the sheriff."

"Right, help with crowd control, that sort of thing," said the guest. "If you need me, I'll be right outside."

Eric nodded absently. Moving quickly across the floor, he tried to avoid trampling the evidence. A nearly impossible task, considering the volume of blood in the room.

At the bedroom door, he braced himself, then flipped on the light. Except for a smear of blood on the carpet leading to the bathroom, the bedroom looked clean. The bed was made. Clothes were picked up and put away. Verbiscar must have been up and in the living room when whatever had happened.

Eric found her in the bathroom sitting on the tile floor, leaning against the wall. A hand towel wrapped one wrist tourniquet-style, with an Exacto knife holding the makeshift device in place.

He reached out and pressed his fingers to her neck. There was a faint pulse.

At his touch, her eyes fluttered open. "Eric?" she said, going soft on the *c*.

"What happened to you?" he asked, forcing himself to keep his tone light. From the wound on her wrist, it looked like a suicide attempt. But why start in the kitchen? And why try to stop the bleeding?

"Someone was here," she said in a slurred voice.

He knew he should tell her not to talk too much, to save her strength. Instead he swallowed and asked, "Anyone I know?"

Verbiscar nodded, almost imperceptibly, then she tried wetting her lips with her tongue.

"Who? Tell me who was here," he prodded, grabbing a bath towel and forcing her to lie down. He felt guilty for pushing her to answer him.

Verbiscar struggled to get up. "The tape —"

Eric gently held her down. "Don't try and get up. You're hurt pretty bad. You're in shock. If you want the tape, let me get it for you."

Collapsing on the floor, she sobbed, "It's gone. The tape is gone."

"How do you know? Did someone take it?" he asked, checking the tourniquet. She'd done a good job of stopping the bleeding. When he tried looking at the wound, it gushed blood, so he repositioned the tourniquet.

"Did you give it to the person who was here?" he asked, rolling another hand towel for a pillow.

She tried shaking her head, then scrunched her dark eyes against the pain. Opening them, she stared at the tourniquet binding her arm. "I'm bleeding."

That was an understatement. "We've called for an ambulance."

Verbiscar coughed, and a small burbling sound bubbled up from her throat. She moved her unbound arm to cover her mouth, and Eric watched in horror as blood oozed from a slice in her shirt. Grabbing a washcloth, he ripped open her shirt and applied pressure to the wound. *What had happened here?*

"It's okay," he said. "Help is on the way. You just hang in there."

"He told me to get rid of the tape," whispered Verbiscar. "I didn't listen. I never listen."

"Who?" said Eric. "The person who was here? The person who did this to you?" His mind flashed to the footprints.

Verbiscar's head lolled to the side, and he felt for a pulse. Thready, but there. Where the hell was the ambulance?

Verbiscar's eyes fluttered open again. "Eric?"

"I'm right here."

She wet her lips. "Tell Charlie he was right."

Chapter 20

Eric sat on a rock one hundred yards from the cabin and watched the paramedics load Linda Verbiscar into a Flight for Life helicopter. It didn't look good. She was in severe shock by the time the ambulance had arrived, and she'd lost a lot of blood.

Vic had shown up on the heels of the paramedics. The Inn on 34 sat just outside the Elk Park city limits, in the jurisdiction of the sheriff's office.

"Fancy meeting you here," he'd said, when he found Eric in the bathroom with Verbiscar. "Stick around. I'll want to talk to you."

After that, the paramedics had ushered Eric out, and Vic had put Deputy Brill in charge of cordoning off the cabin. No doubt since then, the blood evidence had been trampled, and the tracks in front of the house churned into mud.

For the better part of an hour, Eric occupied himself watching mountain bluebirds hunting for insects in the meadow. In the early morning sun, the azure males flitted above the grass like bits of the mountain sky. The female — gray with a blue wash — were harder to spot, hovering like small helicopters, then diving for insect prey. Eric wished he had his binoculars, but they were in the truck, and he didn't want to go near the cabin. Better to sit on the rock.

Vic stood near the cabin's front door, speaking to the hotel manager. The stocky sheriff shook the old man's hand, then turned, hiking up the slope toward Eric.

"Whew," said Vic, panting by the time he reached the rock. Eric slid over and let him sit down.

"So what happened here, Eric?"

"You want the short version, or the blow-by-blow?"

"The blow."

"*Vell,* after you dropped me off, I discovered I had a message from Verbiscar."

Eric walked the sheriff through the morning. He told him about the tape, about Charlie and Tamara Devlin, about finding Verbiscar. When Eric finished, Vic said, "Whew. I take it the tape is the same one you were talking about last night?"

"*Ja.*"

Vic stared at Eric. "Do we have any idea what was on it?"

"No. All she told me was that it proved Wayne didn't light the fire. She wanted me to watch it, to get my reaction on tape. She wanted an interview. I set up the meeting. I never got to see it." Eric ran his fingers through his hair. "Have you talked to Charlie?"

"He's next on my list." The sheriff rested his hands on his knees and drummed his kneecaps with his fingers. "Any idea who or what she might have captured on tape?"

Eric considered the question. "Probably whoever killed Wayne. Doing what, I don't know."

"Okay, son, I'll bite. If, and I mean *if* . . . we have no proof that he was . . . but, if Wayne was murdered, who do you think did it?"

Eric nodded, shifting his weight on the rock to look at Vic more easily. "My list is dwindling."

"I want everyone that ever skimmed it."

"At first I wondered about Pacey Trent. I thought Wayne planned to call off the burn, and Trent was so set on it happening."

"But?" prompted Vic.

"Trent couldn't have done it, based on the timing of the second fire. He was accounted for at all times on the burn site."

"Go on."

"Then there's Nora Frank. She wanted Wayne's job, and she disappeared for a while during the burn. She was gone almost an hour and had access to the ATVs in the maintenance shed near the burn site."

"Anyone else?"

"Lark wondered about Jackie."

Vic cocked his head, donning a thoughtful expression. "She certainly had motive."

Eric stood up. Talking about Jackie as a suspect made him uneasy. It wasn't that he even liked her that much. She tended to be prickly and standoffish. But she was Wayne's wife. Not a surrogate mother in the same way Wayne had served as a surrogate father, but more like a tolerated family member. Someone you afforded loyalty by virtue of relationship.

Eric jammed his hands in his pockets. "Why do you say that?"

"The investigation team got Wayne's autopsy report back," said Vic, sitting up straight and stretching his legs out in front of him. "Wayne had Alzheimer's disease."

Eric's stomach muscles tightened. He felt like he'd been gut kicked.

"It explains a lot about his recent behavior," said Vic. "And it seems to have solidified the case against him."

Alzheimer's. "Did Jackie know?"

"I would assume so. He'd been seeing a doctor in Denver for the past year."

"Wayne might not have told her."

"Maybe. Except, you know what they say, if you can worry about having Alzheimer's, you don't have it. It's usually a family member who recognizes that something's wrong."

Eric wondered why Jackie had lied to

him. To protect Wayne? Or to protect herself and Tamara? A diagnosis like that could have forced Wayne into an early medical retirement, which would have cut his benefits.

"Anyway, I crossed her off the list, because I talked to her at home twice the morning Wayne died."

"By telephone?"

"*Ja*, why?"

"Phones can be forwarded."

"She was at home," said Eric. "Besides, Lark saw her in the Warbler at nine-thirty. She wouldn't have had time to get up on the mountain and back."

Vic cocked his head, then after a moment or two, said, "You got any more on your list, or are we through?"

"There are four more," said Eric. "The two boys from the Youth Camp — ruled out because of the fusees. They would have used one of Wayne's to start the Eagle Cliff Fire. And at the very least, they would have stolen the ones he had on the mountain."

Vic grinned. "You've got them pegged."

"Then, there's Forest Nettleman and Gene Paxton."

Vic frowned at the mention of Nettleman. "What's Forest got to do with this?"

Eric pushed his hands deeper into his pockets, playing his fingers along the seam at the bottom. "He's anti-burn, but you know

Forest. For him, the end sometimes justifies the means."

Vic nodded.

"He and Linda Verbiscar were working together, producing an IMAX-style movie for the center. The film needed fire footage. Verbiscar even hit the list before . . ."

Vic slapped his thighs, and stood up. "And Paxton's motive is self-explanatory. The insurance money."

"I don't think either one of them has an alibi."

Vic's eyes narrowed. "You leave the investigating to me. Do you hear me?" He pointed his finger at Eric. "After what happened here tonight, it's obvious someone got too close to the truth."

Eric let the order hang and laced his next words with sarcasm. "Aren't you worried about jurisdiction?"

"Covered," said Vic, jerking his head toward the cabin. "I'm serious, Eric. Stay out of it."

Eric waited for his frustration to dissipate, then asked, "Did you see all the tracks?"

Vic's eyes narrowed. "What tracks?"

"They were all over the place," said Eric. "Footprints and ATV tracks, both in front and in back." As he spoke the words, Eric realized what had happened. The sun had come up. The sun had warmed the earth and obliterated the evidence, just like the paramedics had obliterated the evidence while rescuing Linda Verbiscar.

Eric slumped back down on the rock. "I'm tired."

"Me, too," said Vic.

Eric hung around until Vic finished interviewing Charlie and Tamara. The cameraman admitted knowing about the tape, but denied knowing who or what was on it. Tamara didn't know anything. She simply cried and begged them not to tell her mother where she'd been.

Lark heard the knock and considered hiding. She was content to be ensconced at the kitchen table with a mug of coffee and the morning paper. She was comfortable in her flannel pajama bottoms and T-shirt. She contemplated ignoring the summons, then caved in. It was probably Velof with the crisis du jour.

Padding across the sun-warmed linoleum, she flung open the door and was surprised to find Eric leaning against the door frame. Self-consciously she fingered her braid, still feathered from last night's sleep. "Good morning," she said.

"Morning." His eyes took assessment of her attire. "Any chance for a cup of coffee?"

"Sure, it's already made." When he stepped inside, she noticed the blood on his hands. "Oh my God, Eric. You're bleeding."

The concern in her voice seemed to embarrass him. "No, it's not mine."

"Then whose is it?" she asked, horrified by the streaks of red blood smearing his hands. "I'd say it's a good thing I know you."

He laughed, a tight, strained release that tugged at her heart. "It's Linda Verbiscar's blood."

"Oh, in that case . . . follow me." She led him to the laundry room and pointed to the wash tub. "What happened?"

"You want the short version, or the blow-by-blow?"

"I'll make us some breakfast." He gave her the short version, while she poured him a cup of coffee.

"So, let me get this straight," she said, peeling bacon strips into a skillet on the stove. "Linda Verbiscar claimed to have a tape that proved Wayne didn't light the Eagle Cliff Fire."

"Right."

"The tape is missing."

"Right again."

"She's in the hospital —"

"And may not pull through."

"And no one knows what was on it."

"You've got it."

"So who do you think took it?" asked Lark, grabbing an onion out of the wooden bread bowl on the counter. Slicing the ends off, she peeled its skin into the trash.

Eric crossed to the stove. "Nora Frank. Forest Nettleman. Or Gene Paxton," he said, turning the strips of bacon in the pan.

Lark's eyes teared from chopping the onion, and she flipped on the cold water, rinsing her hands. "Linda Verbiscar wouldn't have been stupid enough to try blackmailing someone, would she?"

"There were others who knew about the video. She wanted interviews."

The smell of bacon permeated the air. Lark's mouth watered. Drying her hands, she broke four eggs into a bowl, added a splash of milk to the bowl, and whisked the mixture into a yellow froth. "Do you know who else she called?"

"I haven't a clue."

"How about Charlie? Did she confide in him?"

Eric shook his head.

Popping two slices of bread in the toaster, Lark grabbed plates and glasses from the cupboard and carried them to the table. "Tell me Vic is at least going to check out Paxton and Nettleman."

"*Ja,*" replied Eric, taking the bacon out of the skillet. "Do you want the onions in here?"

Lark nodded. "There's a can for the grease under the sink."

Eric rooted around under the sink, drained the grease into the can he found, and tossed the onions into the skillet. "Vic said he was going to ask some questions. From what he told me, it would be hard to convince a judge to issue a search warrant only on the basis of hearsay evidence."

"What about the tracks you saw around the cabin?"

"Gone with the morning sun. Any that might have survived, the emergency crew had pretty well trampled." Eric stirred the onions, then added the eggs. Lark carried the bacon to the table.

After juggling everything to the table — toast, jelly, butter, juice, eggs, and silver-ware — and they had sat down across from each other at the table, Lark slathered a piece of toast with jelly and asked, "So what's your next step?"

"You know me pretty well."

"Yeah, well, that has its good and bad points."

He grinned at her, his brown hair rumpled from being outdoors, his blue eyes twinkling. "More good than bad, I hope."

Lark felt her face flush. *Considerably more good,* she thought, but she wasn't going to tell him that. Their friendship was moving toward something else, but slowly, and she was content with the pace. His friendship mattered to her, and she didn't want to jeopardize that friendship by reading romance in where it didn't belong.

"I told you about the fusees, right?" asked Eric.

Lark nodded, taking a bite of her toast.

"Then there's the missing psychrometer."

Lark set down her toast. "It didn't turn up in the truck?"

"No." Eric shook his head. "He had a special one he carried, and it wasn't in the office. I asked Jackie about it, and she didn't even know what I was talking about."

"Then where is it?"

"I think it's up on Eagle Cliff Mountain." Eric pushed the eggs around on his plate with the fork. "The investigation team issued a quick report on what happened. I think they went up there with some preconceived notion of what they'd find and overlooked something."

"Are you going up there?" asked Lark.

"*Ja*," he said, taking a mouthful of eggs.

"I'll go with you."

"That's not a good idea," Eric said, pushing away his plate. "Not after what's happened to Verbiscar. Someone's frightened, and I don't want you getting in the way."

Lark placed her napkin on the table, then stood up to clear the dishes. "In the way of what?"

"You know what I mean, Lark." His eyes riveted on hers. "It might be dangerous."

"For you, too." She reached for his plate.

"Besides, you're forgetting something. We don't know anything."

"Yet," he replied.

After cleaning the kitchen, Lark telephoned the Drummond and told Stephen Velof that she wasn't coming in. Eric called Nora. He hadn't expected her to answer, but she picked up on the first ring.

"Well, well, if it isn't our local celebrity," she said.

Apprehension stirred in his guts. "What are you talking about, Nora?"

"Don't be modest, Eric. I'd guess by now everyone in Elk Park has heard about your early morning adventures. How does it feel to be a hero?"

His mind scrambled, trying to figure out what she knew, and how she knew it. When he didn't respond, she continued, "KEPC-TV Morning News. They did an in-depth report on Linda Verbiscar and showed a great picture of you sitting on a rock. You looked appropriately dejected and everything." There was a pregnant pause. "Just to satisfy my curiosity, Eric, do you mind filling me in on how you ended up the rescuer?"

Her tone implied impropriety, and the insinuation annoyed him. As far as he knew, the only one who'd been playing around at the inn was Tamara Devlin and Charlie.

"No comment," he said, choosing not to engage.

"Smart man," said Nora, "considering the buzz is you're the prime suspect."

He visualized her leaning into the conversation, her elbows planted on the gray metal desk in Wayne's office. Nora hadn't wasted a moment moving in. Eric's grip tightened around the receiver. If Nora was trying to bait him, she was doing a good job.

Eric refused to bite. "I was calling to let you know I wouldn't be in the office today. I'll take care of the birds at the Raptor House, but afterward I plan to do some field-work to get ready for the fire impact study."

"Really. Are you sure this 'field work' doesn't have anything to do with your fusee theory?"

Damn, how did she know about that? KEPC-TV hadn't been on site in Bellville. "I don't know what you're talking about."

"Don't play dumb, Linenger. The news reporter interviewed Brill. He coughed up your late-night adventures and spilled the beans on your twenty-four count hypothesis. My, but you've been busy." Nora chuckled. "I'm wondering, Eric, can you guess how many fusees I carry around with me?"

Eric worked to keep his voice even. "Make fun if you want, Nora. It's a good theory."

"Hey, we could develop an NPS game show. And now," she intoned sarcastically, "let's play, 'Estimate the Fusees.' "

Anger brought Eric to his feet, and he paced the length of the cord. "Can we get back to business?"

"Sure thing," she said, amusement still lacing her voice.

"I need to map the burned areas for the impact studies," he said. "The sooner it's done, the sooner we can start assessing the effect of the burn." Eric paused, then shot a dagger of his own. "Wayne would have offered, but I'd welcome your help."

"Not a chance, Linenger," she replied. "Take care." Then, she banged down the phone.

Chapter 21

The day had warmed up into the sixties by the time Eric and Lark headed out. The sun blazed down from an azure sky, and the smell of pine hung heavy on the breeze.

Passing Prospect Point, with Eagle Cliff Mountain rising above them, Eric slowed the truck and searched the side of the road for the pullout where Wayne Devlin had parked his truck.

According to Tres's description, the narrow pulloff was sheltered by trees and branched off on the right-hand side of the road. Eric shifted his gaze back and forth from the asphalt to the right-of-way, while Lark kept her nose pressed to the window.

"There," she said, pointing to a shallow opening in the trees. "Is that it?"

Eric braked and yanked the wheel. The truck bumped, straddling the shallow ditch, then came to a stop at the side of the road.

The gap in the trees opened into a small clearing, but the number of days since the truck disappeared, combined with the recent snow, worked against them. Their search for signs that Wayne's truck had been parked there was futile. The moisture had caused any crushed vegetation to regenerate. Short grasses blanketed the earth, dotted with patches of alpine forget me nots and blue columbines. Giant trees towered toward the sky. Any imprints left on the land by any others had been erased.

Eric was about to abandon the search, when his eye picked up nicks in the dirt near the road. Moving closer, he knelt down. Several sets of tire tracks marred the edges of the ditch.

"Over here," he called out.

Lark walked toward him and hunkered down. Her thin-boned fingers explored the indentations in the dirt. "Are they from a pickup?"

"These are," said Eric. He pointed to a set of tracks clearly matching those left by his NPS truck in axle width and tire size. "But these . . ." He broke off and studied another, smaller set. "These look like they came from an ATV."

"Did Wayne use one?"

"He owned an ATV. He used it for packing meat when he hunted. But it's illegal to ride them up here."

Lark shrugged. "Maybe he bent the park rules."

"He wouldn't," said Eric. "Not Wayne."

"You're sure?" she asked. "Even if it meant stopping a burn he didn't believe in?"

Eric sat back on his heels. Bucking policy

established to protect the land, in order to protect the land, smacked of "the end justifies the means" logic reserved for people like Forest Nettleman, not Wayne. Wayne was a man who played by the rules, even if it stacked the odds against him. He was a man of integrity.

"Even then," said Eric.

"But didn't you say you saw ATV tracks in the area where you found Wayne's body?"

"I did." His thoughts flashed to the marks in the grass this morning at the Inn on 34. "And I saw them in front of Linda Verbiscar's cabin."

Lark's eyes widened. "In that case, which of the people on the suspect list own or have access to an ATV?"

Eric tugged at a blade of grass. "We don't have too many suspects left. Between Vic and I, we've bumped everyone but Nora Frank, Gene Paxton, and Forest Nettleman off the list."

Movement overhead drew his gaze. Above them, a hawk carved slow, wide arcs in the air. Dark bars marked the wings' undersides. Reddish-brown with a streaked, creamy breast, the bird sported the characteristic speckled, reddish belly band and rusty-red tail of the red-tailed hawk. He hunted with abandon. Of all the birds, except maybe the woodpecker, the birds of prey benefited most from a fire. The barren landscape exposed the smaller, weaker creatures, serving them up for the larger animals that were higher up on the food chain.

"Keeer!" called the bird.

A shiver coursed along Eric's spine.

"You know, it could have been a tourist," said Lark.

From the tone of her voice, Eric knew she hated suggesting the obvious.

"An opportunist," he said, trying on the idea. Ruling out the Youth Camp boys, why would anyone bash Wayne over the head, light the forest on fire, and steal a psychrometer? The humidity gauge was the only thing missing. He pushed himself to his feet. "No, I think it's someone more cunning and devious."

Lark stood up, too. "How about Nora, then? Would she have had access to an ATV?"

"It's possible." Eric moved toward the truck. "The NPS owns several. Sort of a dichotomy of philosophy, but they're used for moving stuff around in certain areas of the park. There is — or should I say was — a maintenance shed near the fire line. There might have been one there."

"How about Forest?"

"I have no idea." He doubted it, knowing Nettleman. Forest was more the limo type. "But Paxton had one. He kept it parked next to the Shangri-la office, with the keys in the ignition."

"Which means anyone could have borrowed it," said Lark.

Another wrinkle Eric hadn't considered.

He grabbed their gear from the truck, pitching Lark her day pack. In place of the heavy firefighter equipment, they had both gone smaller, packing only the bare essentials — bandana, granola bars, bottled water, sunscreen, lip balm, and binoculars.

Eric stuffed his sweater inside his pack and slung it over his shoulder. Lark cinched her sweatshirt around her waist.

It felt good to climb, and Eric set a brisk pace up the mountain. They headed south, hiking along the narrow deer trail that led away from the clearing. The well-trodden path wound in and around the pine trees dotting the hillside and through fields of columbines blooming in the mountain sunshine. Far below them, the Big Thompson River rumbled toward town, swollen with the runoff from an early spring.

The hillside grew steeper. As the deer path veered away toward the valley floor, Eric wormed his way through the tightly packed lodgepoles on the north slope. Lark stayed close behind, and they climbed until the steep ground forced them to use the trees for handholds and pull themselves hand-over-hand toward the top of the mountain.

Cresting the first ridge, Eric could see the burn one ridge ahead. He was awed by the stark contrast between the unburned and the burned; like someone had drawn a line across a canvas, then painted the lower half of the canvas in color, and the top half in black and white. Below the burn line, the trees grew tall, and birds flitted from branch to branch. Above the burn line, stick-figure trees, wearing ash-colored uniforms, marched like an army across the mountainside, storming the summit of Eagle Cliff Mountain.

"How are you doing?" he asked Lark, pulling out his water bottle and taking a swig. The cool liquid bathed his throat, dry from exertion.

"I'm hanging in there," said Lark, bending over and clutching her waist. Her single braid swung close to the ground. "This is brutal."

"*Ja,* but I can see our destination."

To get there, they simply had to work their way down the back face of the ridge they'd just climbed and hike up the north face of the next.

The back face was a gentle-sloping south face, with a more open landscape of ponderosa pines and Douglas firs, and the going was easy until they crashed into a gully full of shrubs and bushes. There, the vegetation grew so dense in places they were forced to backtrack and search for another route. More than once, Eric wished he'd brought his Pulaski. Then, the vegetation morphed again, back to stands of densely packed lodgepole.

When they reached the edge of the burn, Eric stopped. The forest spread before them, stripped of life, the ground denuded of all but charred soil and charred vegetation. Once-majestic trees stood like skeletons against a gray backdrop of ash. No squirrels scampered or chattered. No birds sang. Only the call of the hawk hunting broke the silence.

The moonscape stretched to the left and right, and Eric struggled to get his bearings. "I remember rounding a large boulder near the bottom of a gully just before I found his body," said Eric. "I think we're still too far north."

Lark agreed, and they traced the lower edge of the burn. One hundred yards to the south, they found what they'd been looking for. The boulder rose like a ship out of a gray ocean and signaled another border. Below the rock, shrubs singed by the fire still grew in profusion. Above the rock, the charred, sepia-toned landscape stretched to the horizon.

On the other side of the boulder was where Wayne had died. With the thought came a shortness of breath, and Eric forced himself to inhale.

"This is it all right," said Lark, pointing to a piece of yellow crime scene ribbon still anchored to a nearby tree.

Eric stepped around the chunk of granite and stared at the small square of land where he'd found Wayne's body. The ash and earth had been churned into waves of mud by the rescue workers, then frozen into stiff peaks of dirt. Eric had to close his eyes to remember the scene.

Wayne had been lying on the ground a few feet from the boulder. The pack leaned against a tree slightly uphill and to the left of his body.

"Let's start here," he said, pointing to a spot that best matched his memory of the area that had surrounded Wayne's body. "We'll work our way up the hill. Keep your eyes open for anything out of the ordinary."

The two of them combed the hillside, traversing the area back and forth, covering every square inch of ground. They found nothing.

Finally, after they backtracked to the boulder and shrugged off their packs, Lark slumped to the ground and rested her back against the rock. Eric flopped down beside her.

"I was so sure we'd missed something," he told her. "Something to do with the —"

"I know, I know. The extra fusee. You are obsessed with the fusee."

She's right, thought Eric. He was obsessed. But Wayne had been anal, and Eric couldn't shake the feeling they were missing something. Some key piece of evidence. He stared at the base of the tree where Wayne's body had been found, willing his ghost to reveal its secrets. He had held the fusee in his right hand, slightly extended above his head.

Eric twisted around and laid on the ground, positioning himself like the corpse.

"He's losing it," Lark remarked, toying with the end of her braid.

"No," said Eric, excitement driving him to his feet. "From where he fell, he couldn't have lit the pile of slash. The fusee in his hand would have touched somewhere in here, and the pile of slash is there." He pointed to the spot where the ash piled into a mound. "Going by the investigation team's scenario, he set the blaze, then scrambled downhill, slipped, hit his head on a rock, and was caught in the fire."

"I can see that happening," said Lark, sounding somewhat apologetic.

"Except, based on the ash, the fusee in his hand was whole."

Lark sat up straight. "And you don't just throw a spark on a pile of slash and start a fire."

"Exactly. Without a propellant of some sort, the fire would likely smolder awhile."

"The investigation team didn't mention any accelerant," said Lark.

"So, now, we're looking at more than one extra fusee." Eric paced the clearing. "Nora would be the only one who'd routinely carry fusees with her. Or another firefighter. Unless . . ."

Eric retraced his footsteps to where Wayne's hand had rested on the ground. If he was right, they would find it here. He kicked the dirt with his boot, loosening the packed soil.

Lark scrambled to her feet. "What? What are you looking for?

"A nail."

Most flares had one. Firefighters used special fusees, ones that linked together in chains making it easier to light a fire. The average motorist or police officer just wanted to signal trouble. They needed to be able to jam the fusee into the ground and make it stand up, hence the small spike at the bottom. A nail would be rock solid evidence that someone other than Wayne had started the blaze.

It took them a few minutes to find what they were looking for. The small, shiny object had been pounded into the ground beneath the boots of the firefighters.

Bending down, Eric pried the nail free of the ground and held it up, end to end, between his finger and thumb. "I'll lay odds, if we look, we'll find more."

"I guess this clears Nora Frank," said Lark.

"Bummer," said Eric, drawing a laugh from Lark, though deep inside he was glad. He couldn't deny that Nora was ambitious. Or that her drive had clouded her judgment at times. But, he hadn't wanted to believe her capable of murder. He hadn't wanted to believe he was that bad a judge of character. "That leaves us with Gene Paxton and Forest Nettleman."

The idea Nettleman might have murdered Wayne wasn't much more palatable than believing Nora Frank responsible. While Eric didn't know Paxton well enough to form an opinion, he knew Forest Nettleman. The one-time powerful U.S. Representative held a passion for the environment. A passion that had clouded his judgment in the past.

The sunlight receded, and Eric glanced up. The afternoon clouds carried no threat of rain, but at this altitude, without the sun's rays, it grew instantly colder. The shadows deepened, and the trees seemed to close in.

He heard a click. It took a moment for his brain to register, to process the sound. *Metal striking metal.* The sound of a gun hammer striking an empty chamber.

Diving for Lark, he knocked her to the ground before the second pull of the trigger drove a bullet into the granite above their heads. A section of the stone splintered, showering them with fragments. He hovered over Lark, ignoring the tiny shards of granite nipping at his skin, aware of her trembling. Where was the shooter?

His eyes swept the hillside above them.

"Eric?" Lark whispered, as though believing her whisper somehow offered protection. The fear in her voice penetrated his calm, and he pushed her closer to the ground. The shot had come from the north.

"Hey, hold your fire," he shouted, urging Lark to move around to the back side of the boulder.

Another bullet whizzed over his head in defiance of his order. This was no small game hunter, and these weren't random bullets. Someone out there was shooting at them. But who? And with what type of gun?

"Stay low," he told Lark, urging her forward.

"Don't worry," she replied. "Can you see anyone? Who's shooting?"

Their eyes met. It had to be either Nettleman or Paxton.

"Forest, is that you?" yelled Eric.

Another bullet slammed into the rock, this time from the west. The shooter was moving counterclockwise along with them.

"Go," Eric ordered Lark. "Keep moving."

They scampered around the end of the boulder, adrenaline driving them through the shrubs and brush on the downhill side of the rock. Squeezing between the boulder and a gnarled mountain mahogany, Eric felt a tad safer. It would be hard to see them in this cover. Harder yet to hit the target.

"Lark," he whispered, drawing her in close beside him. "I'm going to distract him. I want you to head down the mountain. Go as fast as you can. When you reach the road, get to the truck and radio for help."

Lark clutched his arm, her eyes bright with fear. "I won't leave you."

Eric's hand stroked back an errant strand of her hair. The curl soft in his fingers. "I want you to go." Bending down, he swiftly kissed her. "Please."

She brushed the back of her hand across her lips. "I'm scared."

"Me, too," said Eric, then he looked her square in the eye. "Do you remember how the green-tailed towhee operates? He runs along the ground, with his tail held high, creating a diversion. Like a fleeing chipmunk, he scampers into the bushes and hides. He's safe. But more importantly, he's drawn the predators away from the nest." Eric gripped her shoulders. "Our best chance is if you go and get us some help. Will you do it?"

Lark pursed her lips and nodded.

"Good." Eric positioned himself near the mountain mahogany. "Go on the count of three."

He lifted one finger at a time, his hand gripping a branch of the gnarled mahogany. On three, he signaled to Lark and shook the tree.

A shot ricocheted off the rock above him,

and Eric moved, praying that the shooter wouldn't realize Lark had bolted in another direction.

"Nettleman?" He shouted, drawing the attention to himself. "Or is it Paxton?"

Crouched near the rock, his back pressed to the boulder, Eric waited, knowing he had to move. The shooter had been pushing him in a circular motion. Another fifty feet, and he would round the boulder and be on the side where he and Lark had started. He had cooperated up until now, inching along the rough rock away from the attacker. But, at some point, the shooter would double back, making Eric a sitting duck.

Unless . . . What if the diversion hadn't worked?

The thought paralyzed him. Then a bullet slammed into the rock next to his head. A shower of granite pelted his face, and relief washed over him. *He* was still the target, which meant Lark must have gotten safely away.

Another shot came on the heels of the last, and Eric realized he had to move — or die. Somehow the shooter had gotten below him. For the first time, Eric realized he couldn't continue to move counterclockwise around the rock. A large pine tree snuggled up close to the boulder, preventing him from shinning around the granite. If he tried stepping out and moving around the tree, he'd be an open target.

How many shots had been fired? Not that it made any difference. Without knowing the type of gun being used, it was impossible to know how many rounds the shooter had available. Even if Eric found one of the spent bullets, he didn't know types of ammunition well enough to determine the kind of gun being fired. And there were a variety of magazines available.

Face it, Linenger. You're screwed.

That determined, it was better to do something than die cleaved to the side of a rock. Still squatting, he groped the ground for loose rocks, his fingers plunged deep in the duff. Pine needles and twigs bit his flesh, and rough granite scraped his knuckles. Finally he located three or four softball-sized rocks. He hadn't grown up playing baseball, but he'd learned to pitch softball in college, and he had a pretty good arm. Good enough to make someone think twice about coming too close. Even better, he might be able to convince the shooter he was on the run.

Eric pitched the first rock downhill and to his left.

A bullet slammed into the tree below him.

He pitched another rock, aiming slightly below the spot where the first one had landed. The gun fired, chipping a branch off the silver maple fifteen feet below him.

Eric repositioned himself. The bushes around him crackled, and he sucked in a breath. It was now or never.

He pitched another rock and moved down around the base of the pine tree, staying low to the ground. He heard the shot, then felt the searing heat of the bullet skim his forehead. Blood gushed into his right eye, blinding him momentarily.

Realizing he had to keep moving, Eric clambered to his feet and ran for the safety of the trees on the opposite hillside. Shots rang out. He heard the sound of glass shattering.

Dull thuds in the dirt behind him drove him farther into the woods, until, spent, he dropped to the ground near the summit of the ridge.

Blood puddled and caked on his shirt. The world turned.

He listened, hearing only the static in his head and the sound of blood pounding in his ears. He forced himself to lay quietly, forced his breathing to slow. Closing his eyes, he waited for the world to right itself.

The catch of an engine shattered the calm. The engine revved. He heard the sound of dirt spinning off a wheel, splatting against the bark of a tree. The noise receded, and Eric rested his face on the sun-baked dirt.

Chapter 22

Eric had no idea how long he'd been lying there when he heard Lark call his name. He jerked, scraping his face on the hard earth. The sudden movement made him reel, and he fought the nausea that accompanied the pain.

"Eric!" she shouted. He could hear the anxiety in her voice.

"Up here." He barely choked out the words. Lifting his head off the ground, he tried again. "I'm up here!"

As he sat up, his head reeled. When he tried standing, his legs refused to hold him. Elbows to knees, he cradled his head in his hands.

In moments, Lark appeared, a strand of blond hair loose from her braid falling across her cheek. Her blue eyes were narrowed in concern. Tall, thin, dressed in jeans and flannel, and backlit by the sun, she looked like an angel.

Then Vic loomed behind her, hand on his gun. "You hurt?"

"Not too bad," said Eric, focusing on his feet and discounting the headache. "I'm alive."

Lark's fingers probed the wound on his head.

"It's just a nick," said Vic. "He'll live." The sheriff glanced around. "What happened?"

"We were shot at."

"I can see that. Tell me something I don't know."

Eric told him everything he could remember, up to the point where he collapsed on the ground. "Either the guy couldn't find me, or he ran out of ammunition. I heard a vehicle fire up, and that's the last I remember until I heard Lark shout."

"You need to see a doctor," she said.

"He needs soap and water," said Vic. "Why don't we head up to the Youth Camp? We can talk there and get you cleaned up."

"He *needs* to see a doctor," insisted Lark. "He's lost a lot of blood."

"It's a head wound. They always look worse than they are." Vic extended his hand. "Here, let me help you up."

Standing between Vic and Lark, Eric gimped to the boulder. Collapsing against the knobby surface of the rock, he rested while Vic nosed around and Lark retrieved their packs.

"Thanks," said Eric, when Lark pitched him his. Pulling out the bandana, he soaked it with water from his water bottle, and dabbed at the dried blood on his face.

"Here, let me do that," offered Lark. With

skillful fingers and a feather-light touch, she cleaned the wound on his head.

"Ouch," said Eric, when she hit a sore spot.

"Vic's right. It's not as bad as it looks."

"It still hurts," Eric complained.

"Don't whine." Lark doused the bandana with more water. "Hold still." This time she scrubbed, and he winced.

It occurred to him that Lark had gone for help and only brought back Vic. "What happened after you left?" he asked. "Where's the backup?"

"Probably huffing up the hill." She pushed his head sideways and dabbed the wet cloth against his hairline. "I made the road in record time, but I wasn't sure which direction to go for the truck. I flagged down a passing motorist and used their cell phone. As it turned out, Vic was at the Youth Mountain Camp. He got here quick, so we came on ahead."

"That was brave, or stupid, considering someone was up here shooting at us."

"I was worried." She sounded defensive. "Besides, Vic made me wait down below until he was sure the shooter was gone. We only started looking for you after we knew it was safe." She dropped her arm and sat back on her heels. "I'm glad you're okay."

"I'm glad *we're* okay," he answered.

"Ah hum."

Eric glanced up. The sheriff stood ten feet to their left, slightly around the curve in the rock. "Is this where one of the bullets struck?" he asked.

"Could be," said Eric, unable to see exactly where his hands were. "Several shots hit the boulder."

Stooping, Vic patted his hands on the ground. "Ah." He reached his hand into the duff and retrieved a bullet, holding it up to the sun. "From the looks of it, a .45." He slipped the slug into his shirt pocket. "I found what looks like ATV tracks on the hill over there." He pointed south. "Of course, they'll be darned near impossible to track."

The mention of the ATV triggered Eric's memory. He had heard something. A cracking sound. His mind was blank, like an Alzheimer's victim, and it dawned on him this was how Wayne must have felt sometimes. Like a sieve, things came in and passed through, no longer retained.

Allowing his mind to wander away from the task of remembering, it suddenly dawned on him what he wanted to remember. "Glass! I heard shattering glass."

The sheriff raised his eyebrows. "I suppose there's an off-chance whoever was up here clipped a mirror on a tree. If we can find them, the glass fragments might help us prove we have the right vehicle. Provided, of course, we put our hands on the right ATV."

"It wasn't a mirror that broke," insisted Eric. "I heard a shot, then the glass shattered, then the ATV's engine start. The vehicle was parked when the glass broke."

"You know, son, there are a lot of things up here," said Vic, settling his hands on his hips and scanning the area. "But there's not a lot made of glass. Like, *nada*."

Once working, Eric's mind reeled through the events of the past few days. Wayne's murder. The attack on Linda Verbiscar. The tape. *The camera!* "He shot out the camera."

"The shooter is Forest Nettleman," said Lark and Eric in unison.

"Whoa," said Vic waving his hands in the air. "Hold your horses and back up a little there."

"No, she's right," said Eric. "At the last EPOCH meeting, Nettleman explained to us how the Wildland Center uses videocams to monitor wildlife."

"He vocally condemned the burn," said Lark. "And the rumor is, he's filed a lawsuit against the NPS *and* Wayne Devlin's estate for the damages to the Wildland Center."

"He and Linda Verbiscar would have been the only ones who knew where the cameras were located."

"You're sure of that?"

Eric and Lark glanced at each other, then nodded.

"What about Dorothy?" asked Vic.

Eric grimaced. "She might have," he conceded. "But somehow I can't picture Dorothy MacBean bashing Wayne Devlin over the head."

"Or wielding a gun at me and Eric," said Lark.

Vic chuckled. "I have to admit, that's quite an image." His face sobered. "But what about Charlie, Verbiscar's cameraman?"

Eric had forgotten all about Charlie. "*Ja*, him too."

"So really, anyone who knew about the tape would know about the camera."

"*Ja*."

Pushing back his hat, Vic scratched the sweat-lined ring around his head. "Okeydoke, first things first. Let's see if we can find it. Then, depending on how easy the task, we can determine a course of action."

Eric struggled to his feet. He minced his way around the boulder, keeping one hand on the rough granite to steady himself as he scanned the trees. His head throbbed, but the more he moved, the steadier he felt on his feet. Maybe moving around helped get blood back to his brain.

Once they knew what they were looking for, the camera wasn't hard to spot. Eric found it perched high in the unburned trees below the boulder. Shots had been fired to incapacitate it — one to shatter the glass lens, and one to destroy the cassette holder.

The impact from the second bullet had left the camera dangling at an odd angle, making it impossible to know who was up there today, or where the lens had been pointed on the day of the fire.

Vic marked the location of the glass fragments near the bottom of the tree. "We'll get a team up here to work the area, but I don't expect they'll find too much."

From Eric's perspective, what they had was enough. "Nettleman must have discovered Linda had the tape and put two and two together."

Vic rested a hand on Eric's shoulder. "There's only one problem with your theory, son. Nettleman couldn't have started the Eagle Cliff Fire. He had an alibi."

Eric's head snapped up, and he shut his right eye against the flash of pain. "Nettleman has an alibi? But Dorothy said that he was at the Wildland Center in the morning."

"And so he was. He was also in Boulder by ten-fifteen. He had an appointment with someone who could vouch for him. A therapist."

Lark exchanged glances with Eric. She looked more surprised than Eric. "As in psychiatrist?" she asked.

"No, some New-Age therapy. It seems he's got himself a Reiki master. He wants to 'rid himself of anger, balance his chakras, learn to communicate on a higher plane.'" Vic swirled his hand in the air.

"Anything would be an improvement," mumbled Eric. He tried envisioning Nettleman prone on a table while someone cleansed his energy, but the effort made his head hurt. "I guess that leaves us with Paxton."

"That's a leap. Besides, we have nothing to go on," said Vic.

"We have motive — the insurance money," argued Eric. "We have the nail, the bullets fired, and I know he has an ATV. I saw it."

"Has, or had?" Vic pulled off his hat, jabbing the brim toward Eric while he ruffled his hair with his other hand. "Son, there's no way to tie the nail to Paxton. There's no way to prove he drove his ATV up here. And we don't even know whether Paxton owns a gun." Vic shook his head. "We'd need a warrant to search his place, and no judge in his right mind would issue a warrant based on that sort of circumstantial evidence. Hell, no sheriff in his right mind would ask for one." Vic slumped against the boulder. "I'm not saying Paxton isn't our guy. He might be. But there's not enough evidence here to question him over."

Neither Lark nor Eric spoke. Wind whistled through the trees, felling dead snags. The hawk keened. Branches snapped and popped, sounding like gunshots. If Vic hadn't found the bullet, he might have believed Eric and Lark hallucinated the whole thing.

Finally Lark broke the silence. "Paxton doesn't know that," she said.

Eric and Vic both stared at her.

Clutching at the glimmer of hope, Eric said, "You know, she might be on to something. If we could convince Paxton there was enough evidence to convict him, he might talk."

"A bluff?" Vic squinted and rubbed his fingers and thumb along his jawline. Eric could tell the idea appealed to the sheriff.

"I see only one problem with that," said Vic.

"What?" Eric braced himself for disappointment. "Jurisdiction?"

"No, I took this call as a courtesy to the Larimer County sheriff. And the case ties back to Linda Verbiscar, which falls under my auspices. I'm covered there."

"Then what?" demanded Eric.

Vic jammed his hat back on his head and elbowed himself off the rock. "How do we find Paxton? Last I knew he was living at Shangri-la. In case you've forgotten, it burned to the ground five days ago."

"Someone has to know where he is," said Eric.

"What about Mandy Hathaway?" asked Lark. "She's his secretary. If she's anything like Velof, she knows where to find him."

Eric nodded. "Lark's right. Mandy would

know." He pushed himself to his feet. "Does anyone have a cell phone?"

"In the patrol car."

"Then what are we waiting for? Let's go."

"I still say, you need to see a doctor," said Lark, falling in behind Eric.

"Later. I promise I'll go."

"Yeah, right," said Lark. "At the very least, you need to wash it with soap."

Vic chuckled. "Isn't that what I said?"

Halfway down the mountain, they ran into Deputy Brill and two officers hiking up. Vic gave them a quick rundown on the situation, then held up the two-inch nail Eric had found. "I need you to search for more of these. Track the ATV if you can, and collect the camera. You might need a ladder."

Brill groaned. "Which means . . . ?"

"I guess one of you has to go back down," confirmed Vic.

Brill sent the other two officers on ahead then led Eric and the others back to the base of the mountain. Eric's headache increased with each jarring step, the steep pitch forcing them to sidestep down the hillside more than once. When they finally reached the road, they came out half a mile upstream from the truck and patrol car.

Brill flashed them a wave and struck out toward his vehicle. Vic, Lark, and Eric turned downhill, skirted the edge of the asphalt, and headed for the patrol car. After radioing the dispatcher, Vic dialed Mandy Hathaway's number.

"Hi, Ben. It's Sheriff Garcia. Mandy around? Huh. Ah huh. Ah huh. Okeydoke. Thanks." Vic clicked off.

"Vell?"

"Seems that a little thing like a fire doesn't stop an enterprising man like Paxton," said Vic. "He's already hauled a new trailer onto the property and set up shop. Ben told me Mandy's at the office. Do you want to drive with me, or follow?" Eric and Lark chose to follow in the pickup. Turning into the subdivision, Eric noticed that the sign marking the entrance to Shangri-la still stood. The huge billboard — paint blistered, blackened by smoke, and sporting one charred leg — still proclaimed, "Buy a Slice of Utopia." Beyond the gate, a scattered group of slab foundations rose from the ashes like the ruins of Pompeii. Houses that once sprawled against the landscape were now piles of rubble. As if in testament to their former grandeur, fireplace chimneys rose out of the charred debris.

In contrast to the ruins, Paxton's new office looked opulent. A double-wide, cream-colored, three-bedroom trailer with thermal-pane windows and a wraparound deck. A small shed stood off to the side, with Gene Paxton's dusty, blue pickup parked next to it. Beside that, was parked a red ATV.

Vic pulled in in front of the office. Eric followed suit. He started to climb out of the truck, when Vic stopped him. "You two, stay here. Let me go in and talk to him."

Eric started to protest, but Vic held up his hand. "Let me see if I can convince him to let us have a look around."

Slouching back against the seat, Eric watched Vic climb the steps to the wraparound deck. "What do you think?" he asked Lark.

"What choice do we have?"

When Paxton answered the door, Eric turned the key to auxiliary power and rolled down the window.

Dressed in clean blue jeans and T-shirt, with a signature baseball cap perched backwards on his head, Paxton looked surprised to see Vic. "Hey ya, Sheriff. How ya doin'?"

"Good, Gene." The sheriff placed his hand on the butt of his gun. "Mind if I ask a few questions?"

Paxton scratched his beard. Leaning out the door, he looked in both directions, then stepped outside and shut the door to the office. "Like what?"

Vic pointed toward the red ATV. "Does that belong to you?"

"No." Paxton shook his head. "It's Mandy's."

Eric glanced over at Lark. "I'll bet he's borrowed it."

"Ever borrow it?" asked Vic.

Paxton jutted out his chin. "Yeah." He peered toward the NPS truck, then shifted his weight from foot to foot. "What's this all about, Vic?"

Vic smiled noncommittally. "Is Mandy here, Gene?"

"She's inside." Paxton sounded wary.

Vic smiled. "Have you both been around all morning?"

Paxton frowned. "You never answered my question, Vic. What's this about? Am I in some kind of trouble?"

Vic pulled the nail out of his pocket. "Have you ever seen one of these before?"

"A nail?" Paxton sneered. "I'm a contractor. I see nails every day."

"This isn't just a nail," said Vic. "It came out of a car flare."

"Okay. So?"

Mandy had stepped to the window, and Vic smiled at her and waved. Eric reached for the truck's door handle. "I can't sit here any longer."

"Where are you going?" Lark asked, grabbing his arm. "Vic asked us to wait."

"I don't wait well."

"Too bad." Her fingers bit into his flesh. "Put your hands on the wheel."

Eric slapped his hands down on the air bag cover. She was right. The only way the bluff would work is if Paxton didn't run scared and call his attorney.

"Do you mind if I have a look around?" asked Vic, jerking his head in the direction of the shed.

Paxton puffed up his chest. "Yeah, I mind. Now, for the last time, what's going on here? Are you looking for something in particular? Am I under some sort of investigation?"

Vic leaned forward. "I tell you what, Gene. We can do this the hard way or the easy way. I can call and have the judge issue a warrant to search the premises, or you can let me take a look around. Your choice. Of course, if I have to bring out a crew, there's going to be a lot more mess. They're a lot more thorough, and they'll want to run fingerprints, that sort of thing. Still, it's up to you."

Eric's lungs burned, and he glanced at Lark. Paxton wasn't the only one holding his breath.

Paxton exhaled, hitched up his pants. "Well, since you put it that way, I guess it wouldn't hurt to let you look around. I've got nothing to hide."

Vic turned and signaled to Eric and Lark. "You two, want to come with me."

"Hey, wait just a cotton pickin' minute. What do they have to do with anything?" asked Paxton, as Eric and Lark climbed out of the truck.

Mandy opened the door of the trailer and stuck her head out. "Is everything okay?"

"Fine," said Vic. "But, I need you to stick around. I have a couple of questions for

277

you." He gestured toward the shed. "This won't take but a sec."

Vic descended the steps with Paxton in tow, and together the four of them walked toward Paxton's pickup truck. The sheriff signaled Eric to check out the ATV.

"Care to open the saddlebags?" Vic asked, pointing to the white mounted toolbox behind the cab of the truck, the one Eric had seen Gene pitch something into the day of the fire.

While Paxton fumbled for his keys, Eric sidled over to the ATV. Reaching down, he laid his hand on the red engine cover. The machine felt warm to the touch. He looked up and nodded at Vic.

Paxton's hands shook as he inserted the small silver key into the truck's toolbox. "There isn't much in here besides tools," he said, pushing back the cover.

"Mind if I look?" asked Vic.

Paxton hesitated, then stepped aside.

Vic checked visually, then reached inside the toolbox and rummaged around. "You're right, there's not much here." He started to pull his arm back, then hesitated. "Oops, wait a minute."

Eric could see the sheriff straining for a better reach. Paxton looked like he planned to be sick.

"Well, what have we here?" said Vic. He pulled back his arm. Clutched in his fist was a long red flare.

Chapter 23

"I can explain," said Paxton.

"I'm sure you can. And, I'm going to give you the chance," said Vic. "But first, I want everyone to wait here for a minute."

Vic headed to the office, holding the fusee like a baton. Paxton shuffled his feet on the ground. "Do you two know what this is all about?"

Lark looked away.

Eric shrugged. "Someone tried to kill us this afternoon."

Paxton's head snapped up. "And the sheriff thinks it was me?"

"Whoever it was rode an ATV, like that one." Eric pointed to the little red machine. "The engine's still warm."

Paxton's eyes grew wide. "I just rode it, but I didn't take it up on Eagle Cliff."

"Who said anything about Eagle Cliff?" asked Lark.

"I just assumed," stammered Paxton.

Vic came out of the office holding a paper bag. He dropped the fusee in the bag, then strode toward them. "Okay, Gene, let's start from the beginning. Where were you this afternoon?"

"Here. I swear." He pointed at Lark and Eric. "Like I told them, I borrowed Mandy's ATV and rode around the property making a list of damages to submit to the insurance company. I can show you the list. I have it in my office."

Vic put the bag on the seat of his patrol car. "And where were you on Friday, the day of the fire?"

"I was here, all day."

"Did you know about the tape?"

The sheriff moved closer to Paxton with each question, backing him against the blue pickup. Paxton's eyes flicked to Eric at the mention of the tape.

"You were at Linda Verbiscar's," Eric accused. "You're the one who took the tape."

Fear leached the color from Paxton's face. "I'm the one on the tape, I'll admit that. But I didn't do nothin' to Linda Verbiscar."

"What was on the tape?" asked Vic.

"I don't know. I never saw it. Verbiscar contacted me and said she had footage of me stacking wood up on Eagle Cliff Mountain the morning of the fire. She wanted me to come forward about what happened up there. You gotta understand, Shangri-la was draining me dry. I figured, if I started a fire, everybody would just think it was a spot fire from the burn."

He hesitated, and Vic urged him on. "But Wayne caught you, and you killed him."

"No. I piled up some wood, that's all."

"So you're saying you never saw Wayne, and you never lit the fire?" asked Lark.

"I did see Wayne. I never had a chance to light the fire." Paxton leaned against the pickup. "Wayne showed up before I got done. I didn't want him to see me, so I ducked into the woods. I figured I'd wait until he'd finished what he was doing, but then someone else came up and I got scared. I figured Wayne had spotted the slash pile and called for backup. I took off and, the next thing I knew, Wayne was dead and Shangri-la had burned to the ground."

"Who came up?" asked Vic.

"I don't know. I didn't see."

"What was Wayne doing?" asked Eric.

"He was swinging some sort of gadget around. Checking the humidity, I guess."

The psychrometer.

"What happened at the inn, Gene?" asked Vic, his voice quiet but firm.

Paxton hung his head. "When I got there, I found the cabin locked up tight. By the tracks, it looked to me like someone else had been there before me. I knocked on the door. No one answered, so I left. I swear, I didn't do nothin'."

"You didn't go inside?"

"No. I'm telling you the truth, Sheriff. I never saw her."

Eric signaled to Vic, and the two of them

stepped to the back of the pickup.

"Wayne's psychrometer never turned up," said Eric.

"Is that the thing Paxton claims he saw Wayne swinging?"

Eric nodded.

The sheriff grinned. "Then if Paxton has it, we could just about wrap up this case."

Vic strolled back to where Paxton stood. "Mind if I take a look around inside the trailer?"

Paxton focused his gaze on the toe of his boot. "Maybe I need an attorney."

"Suit yourself," said Vic. "I've got plenty to get the warrant I need. Have Mandy lock up, and we'll go downtown until I can get ahold of the judge."

Paxton sighed. His shoulders sagged, then he made a sweeping gesture toward the trailer. "What the hell, I don't have nothin' to hide."

The inside of the office building was nicer than the outside. The front door opened into a large living room with a vaulted ceiling and plush jewel-toned carpet, spread wall to wall. Wood cabinets, mahogany furniture, and overstuffed chairs furnished the front area. In the back, couches ringed a rocked-in fireplace.

"Not bad for a man on the verge of bankruptcy," whispered Lark.

Eric agreed. Either the insurance company

had paid off in record time, or Gene Paxton had squirreled some money away.

Mandy hung up the phone when they entered. "Is everything okay?" she asked.

"The sheriff just wants to have a look around," said Paxton. He pointed toward a door on the right. "My office is in there."

Although the room had been converted to an office, mirrored closets still screamed "master bedroom." The room contained a large cherry wood desk spanning the far windows and three burgundy-colored chairs. Framed prints depicting the three styles of houses one could purchase in Shangri-la adorned the walls. A bookcase lined the inside wall, and vines rimmed the archway to an oversized bathroom complete with Jacuzzi tub.

Eric checked out the bookshelves, while Vic walked over to the desk. The sheriff opened the center drawer and rummaged the contents. He searched the desk systematically, until he discovered a VCR cassette in the lower desk drawer.

"What's this?" he asked, holding up the tape.

"I don't know," said Paxton, his voice rising. "It's not mine." He looked toward Mandy for support. Mandy edged toward the door.

"Mandy?" said Vic.

The woman stopped moving. "Yes."

"Have you ever seen this before?" asked the sheriff, waving the tape to catch her eye.

"Nope."

"I see. Well, do you have a VCR machine in the office?"

Mandy nodded. "In the waiting area."

They gathered around the TV, and Vic popped in the tape and hit the play button on the remote. The screen flashed from blue to images of a pair of three-toed wood-peckers constructing a nest. The film was choppy due to the motion-activated nature of the recording. Suddenly, the image changed, and Gene Paxton loomed into view carrying an armload of deadwood.

"This doesn't look good," whispered Lark. Vic shot her a warning glance.

Paxton slumped into a chair, while Mandy chewed on the inside of her lip. Eric watched in fascination as Paxton added to the pile of slash, looked up, then scurried away. The male woodpecker flew in, and Wayne Devlin entered the frame. He walked over and kicked at the pile of wood. A flash of metal caught Eric's eye.

"Freeze it," he ordered.

Vic hit the pause button on the VCR con-trols. "What do you see?"

"There, you can see the psychrometer hanging from his belt." *He did have it with him.*

"Hmm," said Vic, pushing the play button

again. Wayne turned and walked straight at the camera. His sandy hair waved back from his face, and his blue eyes searched the woods. A flash of recognition crossed his face, then he smiled. Raising a hand, he stepped from view. The woodpecker swooped in again, then the film ended.

"That's it?" asked Mandy.

"That's enough," said Vic. "Gene Paxton, I'm placing you under arrest. You have the right to remain silent . . ."

Eric and Lark waited until Brill arrived, then headed back to town in the NPS truck. They left Vic questioning Mandy. Paxton had already been hauled off to jail.

"It's hard to believe what some people will do for money," said Lark. She'd seen it before. "I'll bet when they do a thorough search, they find the gun *and* Wayne's psychrometer."

"But why take it?" asked Eric. That was the one piece of the puzzle that didn't fit.

"For a trophy."

Eric grimaced. "Serial killers do that sort of thing, not weasels like Paxton. His was a crime of opportunity."

Lark turned to watch him drive. "Are you going to go tell Jackie?"

"*Ja.*"

"You don't sound happy."

He knew he should be overjoyed, but for some reason he only felt empty. The focus on finding Wayne's killer had kept him insulated from the truth. Wayne Devlin, the man he'd grown to love as a father, was dead.

"Do you want me to go up there with you?" asked Lark.

"No," said Eric. Too quickly? He glanced at Lark. "I'd like to do this myself."

How could he explain it to her? Going up there to tell Jackie, was his way of saying good-bye to Wayne.

After dropping Lark off at the carriage house, Eric stopped off at his cabin, changed clothes, and cleaned his head wound, then he headed to the Devlins'. Pulling in the drive, he spotted Wayne's two quarter horses near the split-rail fence and wondered what would happen to them. Jackie most likely planned to sell them. Maybe he would make her an offer.

He knocked, and she answered the front door dressed in a black pantsuit with pink trim. Tasteful mourning. With her blond hair tucked behind her ears, she looked happy to see him.

"Eric, come in," she said, beaming, and he realized her eyes looked clear and bright. Her skin carried natural color. She was healing. It seemed too soon, but then his grieving had just begun.

"I've got some news," he said, stepping into the foyer.

"Really?" She led the way into the living

room. He stopped at the door, surprised to discover the flowers filling the nooks and crannies a few short days ago gone. The bird's-nest ferns were tucked back into the fireplace. Colored pillows were angled in the corners of the couches. And fresh candles adorned the mantel, along with some new knickknacks. She gestured for him to sit on the couch. "So, tell me."

He waited for her to lower herself into a chair, then sat down kitty-corner and reached for her hand. "Gene Paxton was arrested today. They think he killed Wayne."

Her color heightened, and two bright spots of color dotted her checks. "They're sure?"

"We think Wayne surprised him lighting the fire on Eagle Cliff Mountain." Eric omitted Paxton's story about the third party. Something about that niggled at him. "We think he attacked Linda Verbiscar, too. Vic Garcia found a tape tucked away in Paxton's bottom desk drawer that shows Paxton building the fire."

"Strange he would keep that," said Jackie, averting her gaze and worrying her fingers in her lap. "I would have destroyed it."

"I don't know," said Eric. "Maybe he got some perverse satisfaction out of watching himself on the tape. Of course, he's denied everything, except building the fire. Even then, he claims he didn't light it, and therefore hasn't committed a crime."

More disturbing was how convincing he had been when professing his innocence. The circumstantial evidence added up, but the more thought Eric gave it, the more it seemed a piece was missing.

"But they have enough to hold him?" asked Jackie.

"*Ja*. It's mostly circumstantial, but the evidence stacks up against him."

"What happens now?" asked Jackie.

Eric rose from the couch and wandered toward the fireplace. "Trent will ask the investigation team to reevaluate their finding. Wayne's pension will be reinstated. And you'll receive Wayne's full benefits. He died on the job, so you should also receive the extra benefits awarded to a widow and school-aged child."

"Will the lawsuits be dismissed?"

"I think so. You may have to petition the probate court, but I doubt there will be any problems." Eric's hand wandered the edge of the mantel. Small memorabilia of Wayne decorated the painted wood — a medal he'd earned in Vietnam, a tiny picture of him with Jackie and Tamara. Eric lifted the photograph and studied it. Tamara was only a baby. Jackie and Wayne looked so much in love.

Jackie stood up and walked toward a small Queen Anne's desk near the doorway. "I don't know what we would have done without you, Eric. Thank you, for everything."

"Don't thank me. I'm just glad you're going to be able to keep the house. And that Tamara can go to college like she'd planned." He set the picture down and started to turn around when his eye caught on a final item. It was tucked away on the far side of the mantel, canted against the wall beyond the candlesticks. *Wayne's psychrometer.*

Eric stepped closer. Picking it up, he turned it in his hand. Engraved on the bottom were the words, "To Daddy, Love Tamara. Merry Christmas."

The missing piece.

Everything tumbled into place. The lie Jackie had told him about the Alzheimer's disease. Paxton's third party up on the mountain. The ATV tracks. The small footprints at Linda Verbiscar's cabin. The reason the psychrometer was missing.

Eric glanced up. Jackie Devlin leaned against the desk, her hands behind her. He held up the psychrometer. She pulled out a small .38 snub-nosed revolver.

"I'm sorry you figured it out."

He stared at her in disbelief. "What are you going to do, kill me, Jackie?"

"If I have to."

"Is that what happened at Linda Verbiscar's? She figured it out, and you tried to kill her, too?"

"I didn't want that to happen. I knew she had the tape. Tamara told me. She found out from that cameraman, Charlie. I didn't know what was on it, but I needed to know what it showed."

Eric moved, and Jackie sighted the weapon. Her hand shook. He raised his hands in surrender. "So you went to see her?" he asked, hoping to keep her talking long enough to figure out what to do.

"She was sleeping. It was easy to break in, but she jumped me when I tried taking the tape. I had a gun, but I couldn't get to it, so I cut her with the Exacto knife I'd used to jimmy the lock. When she came at me again, I was forced to stab her."

"Why didn't you finish her off?" asked Eric, placing the psychrometer back on the mantel.

"Because Gene Paxton came. He didn't know I was there. In fact, he didn't think Linda Verbiscar was there. But that's when I realized who I could frame for Wayne's murder." She laughed, a sharp high chortle. "He made it so easy." She closed her eyes and drew a ragged breath. "Now you've made it hard again."

"But why, Jackie? That's what I want to know. Why kill him?"

"Do you think it was easy living with him?" She stared toward Eric, looking right through him. "The Alzheimer's changed Wayne. There were times he didn't know us anymore." She moved away from the desk and closed the French doors leading to the dining room. "Nora Frank wanted to have him fired. He had two years left, two years. There's no way he could have lasted that long. We would have lost his full pension. Tamara wouldn't have been able to go to college." Jackie latched the doors. "She simply couldn't bear the thought."

Her words triggered a memory. He and Wayne hunkered down behind a bush in a park campground being charged by a mother bear. A mother bear protecting her cub. In the flash of a memory, Eric knew the truth.

Chapter 24

"It wasn't you up on Eagle Cliff Mountain, was it? It was Tamara."

Jackie flashed Eric a thin smile, then gestured for him to sit down. "She did us all a favor, you know. Wayne didn't want to live like that. I couldn't help him. I loved him too selfishly. He told us both, 'the best thing that could happen now, the best thing for all of us, is for me to die. And preferably on the job.' Don't you see, he asked her to kill him. Tamara loved her daddy with a purity of heart only the young can define, and she did what her daddy asked her to do."

"Are you saying she helped him commit suicide?"

"In a sense." Jackie's gun arm trembled, and she braced it with her free hand. "She followed him up there, unsure about his plans, but prepared to help him make it look like he died in a fire. She took an emergency flare from her car."

That explained the nail, thought Eric. "What happened then?"

"Wayne was testing for moisture on an incline, and his balance wasn't good," she said, gesturing toward the couch again, this time with the barrel of the gun. "Tamara pushed him. He fell and hit his head. She thought he was dead, so she started the fire. Then, she stuck the fusee in his hand and left."

Which explained the fusee residue on Wayne's glove.

Eric moved slowly toward the couch. "She murdered her own father, Jackie. She needs help. You both need help."

"What sort of help, Eric? The sort we'd get in prison?" She uttered a brittle laugh. "My baby doesn't belong in prison. She belongs at Harvard or Yale. She was valedictorian of this year's class, or didn't you know?"

Eric knew.

"Put the gun down, Jackie," he said. "Everyone knows I came here to see you. It's over. If you shoot me, they'll know you did it."

"But I can tell them my version of what happened, which means I can still save my baby." Jackie finger teased the trigger. "It's the only choice you've given me."

Eric's eyes searched the room for a way out. Jackie had locked the French doors leading to the dining room, which left only the entrance to the hall open. Unfortunately, she stood between him and there. And while ducking behind the couch might buy him a little time, she had only to squeeze the trigger a second time.

Wait! Jackie had pulled the gun from the

Queen Anne's desk, but who had put it there? Wayne? He had kept loaded guns around the house for protection. He also *always* left the first round blank.

Eric prayed the Alzheimer's hadn't affected Wayne's routines. It was his only hope.

"I'm sorry, Eric." Jackie's eyes shone. Tears trickled down her cheeks. "I didn't know the sacrifices we'd all have to make when I asked you to help us."

Then, she didn't know it was Tamara when she first asked him to help her find Wayne's killer.

"When did you figure it out?" he asked.

"I found the psychrometer in her jeans pocket while I was doing laundry."

The front door opened, and Tamara came in. "Hi, Mama, I'm home."

In a panic, Jackie turned away from Eric. "I'm in the living room, honey, but don't come in here, please. I have a surprise for you. I don't want you to spoil it."

Now was his chance. Eric leaped for the gun.

Jackie whirled back around and squeezed the trigger. The hammer fell with a click.

Eric made another leap. Jackie squeezed the trigger again, drawing back the hammer. He batted her arm to the side. The gun fired.

Tamara screamed, her shrill voice piercing the air. Jackie stared in horror. Tamara hadn't done what her mother had told her. Instead, she'd made a beeline for the living room.

Tamara dropped to the floor, and the gun dropped from Jackie's hand. The woman sank to her knees beside her daughter.

"Tamara. Oh my God, my baby." Jackie stroked her daughter's hair away from her face. "I'm sorry. Oh my God, what have I done?"

Eric pulled into the Beaver Meadows turn-around bright and early. Lark was waiting for him. She sat on the tailgate of her pickup, watching the sun tint the mountains pink in the dawn of the day.

"Coffee?" She held out a thermal mug.

"Thanks." He sipped the dark roast, then scooted up beside her, letting his feet dangle.

"How's Tamara?" she asked, kicking her feet and letting them swing.

"She took a bullet to the shoulder. She'll live."

"Ah," said Lark. "A soap and water wound."

"No, it was worse than that. She needed surgery. And stitches. And she also found herself a good lawyer. From what I hear, in addition to defending her in the criminal trial, she had the attorney file a lawsuit against Jackie for reckless endangerment."

Lark smiled, and sipped her coffee. With

her head bent, the early morning sun warmed her hair to a shade of golden honey. "What's going to happen to them?"

Eric forced his gaze to the meadow. "They're going to jail."

"And Paxton?" Lark pulled her blue flannel shirt closer around her.

"Cold?" he asked, draping his arm about her shoulders. She snuggled in closer.

"You didn't answer my question."

"Paxton gets off."

"Completely?"

Eric nodded. "The way Vic explained it, Paxton didn't commit any crime. He piled wood with intent, but he never lit the fire, and there's nothing in the Colorado statutes that says piling wood is a crime."

"What about the tape Vic found?"

"Jackie Devlin planted it there. Paxton went to see Verbiscar, but he never actually connected."

Lark took another sip of coffee. "So, how is she?"

"Verbiscar?" Eric rubbed his hand up and down Lark's arm. "She's healing. I hear they're going to let her out of the hospital soon. And, apparently, the network is going to give her a shot at the early morning broadcast. Trust me, she'll dine out on this story for years."

A car pulled up to the turnaround, and Eric lifted his arm from Lark's shoulder. The rest of the participating EPOCH members had arrived. Dorothy MacBean and Cecilia Meyer came first, followed by Andrew and Opal Henderson. And, as they unloaded their birding equipment, Harry Eckles showed up with Gertie Tanager.

"Give us the lowdown, Eric," said Andrew. "What exactly do you want us to do?"

"I want us to fan out across the meadow. The purpose of the study is to determine the impact of fire on avian populations. We know that some birds fare better than others after a fire. We expect to see declines in some bird species and increases in others. And, we expect there will be some species that disappear completely and never return."

"Like the green-tailed towhee?"

"That's my fear." Eric looped his binoculars around his neck and picked up his field notebook. "Oh, and, in addition to the birds you spot, if you would, please jot down the types of live vegetation you see, and please make notes of any other wildlife or invertebrates spotted in the area — beetles, squirrels, rabbits." He scanned the faces. "Questions?"

Gertie's hand shot up. "How long do you want us to stay out there?" She gestured toward the meadow.

"Half a day. Longer if you're up for it." He glanced around. "Anyone else?"

No one said anything.

"Let's get going, then." Eric stepped off the berm, and the meadow spread before them — a charred blanket of ash and burned bushes. The late-spring snow had encouraged some of the unburned grass to green up, and spots of the meadow already showed signs of recovery. Too bad the forested area wouldn't rebound as quickly, he thought.

He'd gone thirty feet, then spotted the bush where he'd seen the green-tailed towhee building its nest prior to the burn. The charred branches of antelope bitterbrush stuck up in brittle spikes, ready to be felled by the first puff of wind.

Drawing closer, Eric could see that the back side of the plant was still green. He jotted down the observation, and a flash of movement caught his eye. He studied the bush, and spotted another flash of orange.

"Lark," he called in a stage whisper. "Everybody. Check this out."

The group gathered.

"Remember I told you I was worried about the green-tailed towhee?"

They nodded.

He pointed to the bush. "They stayed." He smiled at the others. "Check it out. They're building a nest in the ashes."

GREEN-TAILED TOWHEE
Pipilo chlorurus
Family: Emberizidea

APPEARANCE: The smallest of the towhees, this bird is quite drab. In good light, it will take on a greenish sheen. Watch for its white chin and distinctive rusty-red cap. The green-tailed towhee has a long tail, and if an intruder approaches, it will scamper along the ground like a small mammal, hoping to distract the predator.

RANGE: The green-tailed towhee is a migratory bird that summers in the western United States from eastern California to central Colorado and Montana to New Mexico. It winters throughout Mexico.

HABITAT: Watch for the green-tailed towhee in the foothills and low brush of the higher elevation scrublands. It is also found in mountain thickets, chaparral, and riparian scrub.

VOICE: Its song is a series of chip notes, *chu-weet-chur, chee-chur*, followed by two or more trills. Its call is a nasal *meewe*. When it is in flight, listen for a long thin buzz, *zeereesh*.

BEHAVIORS: The green-tailed towhee is a monogamous bird that lives either alone or in pairs. It may form loose flocks with other species in winter. A classic double-scratcher, the green-tailed towhee forages on the ground beneath dense thickets by pulling both legs sharply backward at the same time. The green-tailed towhee eats seeds, fruit, and insects and their larvae. Secretive and easily overlooked, it may be detected by the loud rustling it makes scratching for food in the leaf litter. It has a rapid, bouncy flight, and alternates between several quick wing beats and pulling its wings tight to its sides.

CONSERVATION: An uncommon cowbird host, the green-tailed towhee is vulnerable to the loss of habitat due to land clearing, grazing, and development. Studies are now being done to determine the effects of prescribed fire on the species.

About the Author

Christine Goff lives in Evergreen, Colorado, with her husband, three out of six children, two dogs, two rabbits, and flocks of wild birds.

You can visit her website at http://www.christinegoff.com.

We hope you have enjoyed this Large Print book. Other Thorndike, Wheeler or Chivers Press Large Print books are available at your library or directly from the publishers.

For more information about current and upcoming titles, please call or write, without obligation, to:

Publisher
Thorndike Press
295 Kennedy Memorial Drive
Waterville, ME   04901
Tel. (800) 223-1244

Or visit our Web site at:
www.gale.com/thorndike
www.gale.com/wheeler

OR

Chivers Large Print
published by BBC Audiobooks Ltd
St James House, The Square
Lower Bristol Road
Bath BA2 3SB
England
Tel.   +44(0) 800 136919
email: bbcaudiobooks@bbc.co.uk
www.bbcaudiobooks.co.uk

All our Large Print titles are designed for easy reading, and all our books are made to last.